ariel tachna
FALLOUT

Dreamspinner Press

Published by
Dreamspinner Press
382 NE 191st Street #88329
Miami, FL 33179-3899, USA
http://www.dreamspinnerpress.com/

Cover Art by Shobana Appavu bob@bob-artist.com

ISBN: 978-1-61372-522-1

Printed in the United States of America
First Edition
May 2012

eBook edition available
eBook ISBN: 978-1-61372-523-8

To the heroes of Fukushima Dai-ichi, whose willingness to risk their lives to save others inspired this novel.

ARIEL TACHNA
Contemporary M/M Romance at its Finest

Inherit the Sky

"…a well crafted, beautiful book that I would recommend to anyone looking for a love story that takes courage." —Guilty Indulgence
"This story is beautifully, realistically handled." —Joyfully Jay

Her Two Dads

"…one of the most emotionally rewarding and uplifting love stories that I have read in a long time." —Dark Diva Reviews
"This is one of the best books I have ever read."
—Judging the Book by Its Pages

Seducing C.C.

"…a great comfort read." —Blackraven Reviews
"…a seductively sexy and romantic story." —Night Owl Reviews

Out of the Fire

"This story tore at my heart." —TwoLips Recommended Read
"…something in it for just about everybody who has a kink…"
—The Romance Studio

Once in a Lifetime

"… a coming-of-age story that introduces heart-pounding firsts and nostalgic lasts." —¡Miraculous!

http://www.dreamspinnerpress.com

chapter
ONE

WHEN Tropical Storm Elsa aimed its sights at the Texas Gulf Coast, Derek Marshall shrugged and checked his generator to make sure he'd have backup power if they lost electricity for more than a few hours. When the storm was upgraded to Hurricane Elsa, he checked his readiness kit to make sure he had plenty of water just in case the local water system was compromised. When Category 1 became Category 2, he made sure he had plenty of canned goods. When Category 2 became Category 3, he checked the propane tank for his grill. When it became Category 4, he closed his storm shutters and hunkered down with a bottle of tequila to wait it out.

The bitch stalled ten miles offshore, pummeling the Gulf Coast for days, stretching from east of New Orleans almost to Brownsville, spawning storm surges that rolled inward ten miles in places, Derek discovered later. At the time, he was only aware of the pounding winds and the incessant rain. His house was at the highest point in his neighborhood, but when he peeked out between the slats of his storm shutters, he could see the waters rising. His weather radio reported flooding throughout Galveston, Houston, Bay City, and farther west. Government officials warned people to stay inside. The 135-mile-per-hour sustained winds made it dangerous to even think about going outside. If they hadn't followed the advice to evacuate, they needed to stay where they were and hope for the best until the storm passed.

Derek turned off the radio and opened a second bottle of tequila. If he died, at least he'd go happy.

When the winds finally passed and the rain slowed to a drizzle, Derek opened the storm shutters and peered outside with bleary eyes.

Only one in every three houses still had its roof, and the other two in three had lost walls as well when the roofs collapsed. Even drunk as he was, it occurred to him that he was damn lucky to be alive, so he waded through the flooded streets to the houses nearest his, checking to see if anyone else had stayed and, if so, if they'd made it through.

He didn't find any people, but he did find a dog in the rubble of one of the houses, shivering in fear. It came out when Derek called, though, its tail wagging even as it continued to shake. Derek searched through the house as much as he could until he found a couple of cans of dog food. If the owners were in the house, he didn't see any sign of them. "Who the hell leaves a dog alone at home with a storm like Elsa on the way?" he muttered. He sat down next to the dog, heedless of the rain and the rubble. The mutt put its muzzle on Derek's thigh, the trembling finally starting to ease as Derek stroked its head. "It's okay, Fido," he said, keeping his voice soothing. "I'm not going to leave you alone. You're going to come home with me, and I'm going to take care of you. Are you okay to walk? You came out here to me pretty well. If you are, let's get out of the rain and inside where it's drier."

Derek kept a close eye on the dog as they braved the floodwaters between the rubble of the dog's house and Derek's house. The water came up to the dog's belly, but it trotted along beside him trustingly. If Derek hadn't had the dog food in his hands, he'd have picked the animal up, but he couldn't carry both of them, and Fido seemed willing and able to walk. When they reached his house, he cast a critical eye over the roof. He could see shingles missing, but it didn't look like the tar paper beneath was damaged, so he hoped there wouldn't be any leaks. The house had to keep him and Fido safe and dry until the floodwaters went down and the power came back on.

"It's okay, boy," he repeated as they walked into the house. "We made it through the storm. Everything after this is easy." The thought of looters occurred to him, although as dead as the neighborhood appeared, he wasn't sure anyone else had stayed—or survived if they did—but he decided it wouldn't be a bad idea to keep his gun handy. Just in case.

He pried one of the cans of dog food open with a pocket knife because the dog looked too pathetic to wait, and then powered up the generator and unlocked his gun from the safe. The whiff of cool air when the air conditioner kicked in was a relief after three days of unrelenting humidity. Derek plugged his cell phone in and checked idly for reception. To his surprise, he had one very weak bar. And ten new messages on his voice mail.

The first one was a simple request from his mother to call him when the storm had passed. He dialed her number quickly and let her know he was fine, if a little cut off at the moment. When he got off the phone with her, he listened to the rest of the messages.

"Marshall, when you get this message, call me."

"Marshall, where are you? I need you to call me."

"Marshall, where the hell are you? Don't tell me you're still at home."

"Derek Marshall, if you don't call me the minute you get this message, you won't have a job to come back to."

Derek rolled his eyes at that one. His boss at NASA regularly threatened his job, but since Derek was the best robotics engineer in the country, he figured he'd have to do more than not return a call before he'd be out of work.

The remaining five messages, all from his boss, grew increasingly frantic, culminating with, "Derek Marshall, if I find out you stayed at home to wait out this fucking hurricane, I will fucking kill you myself. Call me."

Deciding the string of profanity meant the situation, whatever it was, really did merit immediate attention, Derek dialed his boss's number.

"Where the fuck are you?"

"Hello to you too, Kenneth," Derek said with a roll of his eyes. His boss was short on social niceties at the best of times. Derek didn't know what was going on, but this clearly didn't qualify as the best of times.

"Don't give me that, you bastard. Where are you, and more importantly, where's that piece of junk you call Number Five?"

"If you talk that way about it, I won't tell you," Derek threatened. He'd started building robots after he first saw the movie *Short Circuit*. He'd fallen in love with the quirky robot who saw more than he should have. As a robotics engineer, Derek appreciated the difference between reality and fiction, but it hadn't stopped him from naming his prototype Number Five when he'd started working on it three years ago. "I'm at home, and Number Five is right here with me. What do you need us for?"

"The number three reactor in Bay City is compromised," Kenneth said. "I need your robot and your genius with other people's robots to work with a team to get it under control. The President called NASA specifically asking for our best robotics people."

"There's two feet of water in the streets around my house," Derek said. "Trees down, houses collapsed. There's no way I'm going anywhere, with or without Number Five."

"If I get you there, will you help?" Kenneth demanded.

"If you can get me there," Derek agreed, "but give me an hour before you pick me up, and send coffee. Elsa and I celebrated her arrival with tequila."

"You spent the whole storm drunk, didn't you?"

"How else would you ride out a hurricane?"

"Somewhere safe?" Kenneth retorted. "Be ready in an hour, Marshall. And be prepared to stay awhile."

"What about Fido?" Derek asked.

"Fido?"

"My dog."

"You don't have a dog."

"I do now," Derek said. "He rode out the storm in the house down the street. The damn thing fell down around him. He's mine now."

"Fine. Someone will take care of the damn dog."

"Fido," Derek said. "His name is Fido."

"Someone will take care of Fido."

After setting down his phone, Derek contemplated what to pack. He tossed a few changes of clothes in a bag. He could wash them if he needed to at some point. Up in his workshop, he packed Number Five carefully in the custom-designed case he'd ordered once he'd determined the size he intended the robot to be. Then he considered the rest of his equipment and what little he knew of the situation. A compromised nuclear reactor meant radiation, and that meant degrading circuits. He grabbed a duffel and started filling it with the tools and replacement parts he had on hand to keep Number Five running and possibly to upgrade any other robots at his disposal. If he had to, he'd build another one or two. The cost of a few robots would be far less than the cost of cleaning up from a core breach and meltdown so close to Houston. He looked around one more time, but everything left was a duplicate of what he'd already packed. He hefted the duffel over his shoulder and carried Number Five down to the foyer of his house. His mother called it self-indulgent to have as much space as he had just for himself, but then his mother thought that about a lot of things in his life. He didn't even want to think about what she'd say about the collection of gay porn on his laptop or the gay skin magazines by his bed. Speaking of which, he'd gotten a new one recently. He should take that with him. He could put the pinups in his room wherever he was staying to make it a little more pleasant. There probably wouldn't be anything else to do with his downtime but whack off.

His phone rang again while he was adding the magazine to his laptop case. "Are you ready?"

"As I'll ever be," Derek said. "Number Five is packed along with as much of my equipment as I can carry. I'm a little more sober now. What's going on?"

"I've already told you all I can," Kenneth replied. "You'll be briefed when you get there. They're trying to avoid widespread panic and so are keeping information classified as much as possible."

That didn't sound promising. "There are escape protocols in place if this goes south on us?"

"It's already gone south," Kenneth said. "We're trying to keep it from going nuclear."

"Well, shit," Derek said. "That's not encouraging."

"That's why we need Number Five," Kenneth said. "He can go where people can't, and you've got him so fine-tuned he can do anything you could do with your hands and more."

If Kenneth was complimenting Derek's robot, it was beyond bad. "Have they shut down the core at least?" Derek didn't know much about nuclear power, but he knew that much.

"I've told you all I know. The helicopter is leaving now. It'll be there in fifteen minutes to pick you up. Good luck, Derek."

From the sound of it, he'd need it.

"Come on, Fido." He urged the golden brown mutt out of the laundry room, where it had taken shelter. "We're going on a trip."

In closer to ten minutes than the fifteen Kenneth had predicted, the *chop-chop* of a helicopter's rotors shook the windows in the house. Derek dashed out beneath the spinning blades. "Turn it all the way off," he shouted to the pilot. "I've got a petrified dog in the house and no crate because he's a rescue. We can strap him in, but I don't think he'll come with the noise."

"Mr. Marshall, we don't have time for this."

"Then find someone else with my skills who's stupid enough to agree to this," Derek said, turning away. "Fido and I will stay here where it's safe."

"I'd hardly call this safe. What if looters come through?"

Derek pulled back the edge of the jacket he was wearing. "They'd be in for a nasty surprise. Now, are you turning this thing off, or am I going back inside?"

The pilot looked like he wanted to argue more, so Derek turned around and sloshed back toward the house, grateful once again that he'd bought the house on the hill, such as it was.

"Mr. Marshall, wait! It'll take a minute for the rotors to stop."

Derek waved to show he'd heard the man. "I'll bring my equipment in the meantime."

He went back inside and petted the dog reassuringly. "We're just going to take a ride somewhere safe and warm, okay, Fido? Let me put my bags in the chopper and I'll come back for you."

Fido had other plans, following Derek out into the drizzle. When he put his bags in the helicopter, the dog whined pitifully. "We're just going to lock the doors, and then we can go," Derek promised. "I won't leave you behind."

The dog stayed right at Derek's heels as he locked the door and hoped he'd have a house to come back to when he finished this project for Kenneth. "Come on, Fido."

They slogged back to the helicopter. Derek helped Fido jump in and climbed in after him. He strapped the dog to one of the seats and then fastened his own seatbelt. Taking the headset the pilot offered him, he waited for the helicopter to take off before asking, "Where are we going?"

"South Texas station, unit three," the pilot answered. "There's a team waiting for you."

"And the dog?"

"I guess you'll have to take him with you."

That wasn't what Derek had had in mind when he'd told Kenneth he expected someone to take care of his dog, but it would have to do until he could get Kenneth on the phone again.

They spent the next hour in relative silence. Derek looked down at the devastation from the hurricane, the sight killing what remained of the tequila buzz. Where once there had been a thriving city and port, industry and commerce, now there were floodwaters and rubble, only the occasional building still standing. It made him realize how lucky he was to still be alive. He peered toward downtown Houston and the Texas Medical Center, but the lingering clouds and rain blocked his view. He hoped that was the reason, that they still stood, hidden by the weather rather than flattened by the storm.

"How bad is it?" he asked eventually.

"It makes Katrina look like a cakewalk," the pilot said. "Maybe one in five buildings is still standing, and even most of those are damaged. I've never seen anything like it. And if you can't stop the problems at unit three, there won't be any coming back because it won't be safe."

"Let's not borrow trouble, okay?" Derek said. "We've got enough real trouble as it is."

"You don't think damage to a nuclear reactor is real trouble?"

"I didn't say that, but it isn't Chernobyl yet or they wouldn't be sending us in to work on it. If we can get it back online, at least we'll have power to begin rebuilding."

The sound the pilot made was doubtful, but Derek let it go. He didn't need to convince the pilot. If the rest of the team was as negative, that would be a different matter.

The power plant came into view, the three units easily visible. The first two stood silent and still without the usual white smoke from the water vapor. Shutting down those two plants had clearly gone according to plan, just as Kenneth had said. The third unit, though, belched dark gray smoke constantly. The pilot put the copter down near the troubled unit.

"Turn the engine off."

"Look, Mr.—"

"Turn the fucking engine off," Derek shouted through the headset. "You want to get out of here, so turn it off, let me get my supplies unloaded, and then you can get the hell out of Dodge."

Derek took the headset off rather than listen to the pilot's vitriol. After a moment, the engine noise faded, leaving only the sound of the rain on the metal frame. Derek hopped out and unfastened Fido. Then he hoisted his gear. "Come on, Fido," he said, walking toward the power plant as fast as he could under the weight of his equipment.

He was halfway to the only entrance he could see when the door opened and a man stepped outside. From what he could tell through the gray drizzle, the man was, like himself, in his mid-thirties, although the dress shirt buttoned all the way to the top was something Derek wouldn't be caught dead wearing outside a business meeting with the NASA directors, and even then he usually lost the tie and opened the top button when they got down to serious business. "Here, take this." Derek passed the bag with his clothes to the other man. "I'm soaked through, and some of this equipment is moisture sensitive."

The man, Indian or Pakistani to judge by his coloring, scowled but took the bag. "The dog can't come inside."

"Then I'll take my bag and head home. I already told my boss I wasn't abandoning him after his previous owners left him alone in the storm."

"Fine," the man said with a huff, "but keep him out of my way."

"Look, bud—"

"Sambit," the man interrupted. "My name is Sambit Patel."

"Look, Sam," Derek said, not even trying to pronounce the foreign name, "I'm here with my robot out of the goodness of my own heart, so get rid of whatever bug crawled up your ass and died and tell me what needs to be done. Fido and I would like to go home."

"First, my name is Sambit, not Sam. Second, Mr. Marshall, I suggest you leave your attitude at the door. I'm here out of the same goodness of heart, as you call it, as you are. The employees of the plant who were on duty are either dead or in the hospital with injuries from the tornado that struck along with the hurricane and flooding. The off-shift workers were evacuated along with the rest of Bay City, and no one knows where they are at the moment." Sambit must have gotten a more thorough briefing than Derek had if he knew Derek's name. Derek wondered what else he knew that Derek didn't.

"So if I'm the robot guy, then who are you?"

"The nuclear engineer," Sambit replied. "I teach in the nuclear engineering department at Texas A&M."

"So you don't know any more about this plant than I do."

"I know quite a lot about nuclear power plants." Sambit crossed his arms over his chest, the posture so defensive Derek nearly laughed in desperation. They were so screwed.

"So what's the status of the core?"

"It is compromised," Sambit said. "Beyond that, I don't know. The power went out ten minutes ago."

"There has to be a backup. A system this critical would have a UPS backup system—uninterruptible power source," he added for Sambit's benefit. "Plus separate backup generators in case the UPS fails."

"I know what a UPS backup system is," Sambit snapped. "I may deal with theory more than practice these days, but my students have to be prepared to work in plants just like this one."

Derek resisted the urge to roll his eyes, and set down his gear. "Come here, Fido." He ignored Sambit while he petted the dog's head a few times, settling it in yet another new location in a matter of hours. "Stay here, okay? Sam and I are going to find the light switch, and then we'll come back for you."

The dog circled twice and curled up in the corner of what was clearly the break room. "Do you at least have the passwords for the computers once we find the backup power?"

"What passwords?"

"You don't seriously think a system like this one is going to operate without password protection to keep terrorists from hacking into the system and causing a meltdown, do you?" Derek rolled his eyes at the other man's ignorance. "Once we get the power back on, we'll call the plant managers and see if we can get the log-on information. You're the nuclear engineer. How long do we have before it gets critical?"

"It depends on how badly the core has overheated," Sambit replied. "Without the computers, I can't tell for sure."

"Well, fuck," Derek muttered. "Is there anything you do know?"

"I know you have a bad attitude and a foul mouth."

"Like that's news. Is there anything you do know about the status of the plant?"

"Not much, but hopefully we will get the computer system online soon."

Derek cursed again and dug in his bag for a flashlight. "Do we need to worry about radiation?"

Sambit handed Derek a dosimeter. "The levels are safe here. Whether they are safe elsewhere...." He shrugged as he trailed off.

Derek clipped the device to his belt. "If I were a backup generator, where would I be?"

"Why are you asking me?"

"I'm not," Derek said. "I'm thinking out loud. Stop distracting me."

He walked out of the staff room and searched for a stairwell. Once he found one, he headed down. "That explains the backup power being off," he muttered when, after four steps, he hit water. "Who puts a basement in a building a few miles from the coast? If the generators are down there, we're fucked. Where the hell are the schematics for this place? The backup generators should be in another building entirely, but I'd expect there to be controls around here somewhere."

"I don't have them," Sambit said. "I already told you that."

"It was a rhetorical question," Derek snapped back. "Look, why don't you go hang out in the staff room? When I get the power on, we can figure out the rest."

"It's not safe to be here by yourself," Sambit insisted. "What if you get hurt? I won't even know where you are."

"Fine, but shut up so I can concentrate."

They headed back into the corridor and worked their way through the rooms in the control section of the power plant. Not finding anything, Derek headed to the outlying buildings, searching each one until they found the backup generators. Derek studied them carefully, resisting the urge to look at his dosimeter every few seconds to see if the numbers had changed. Based on the systems at NASA, he would have expected them to turn on automatically when the battery system failed, but this wasn't NASA so maybe the protocols were different. Or maybe the generator was faulty and they were totally screwed. There was only one way to find out.

He checked the dials and gauges, fiddling with the diesel intake until the first generator sputtered to life. "Maintenance protocols are there for a reason," he muttered at no one in particular. "Okay, Sam. Let's get the computers on so you can tell me where to send my robot and what to do when he gets there."

They went back into the main monitoring room. Sambit turned on the central computer and waited for it to boot up. It powered up willingly enough, but the moment it came online, it demanded a password. "We could try calling the hospital," Sambit suggested. "The plant manager was in serious condition, but he did survive the storm, according to my briefing. He might be in good enough shape to help us."

"Call and see if you want." Derek cracked his knuckles and started typing. He'd have liked to think the security software for the plant would require the users to have a strong password, but he'd seen that fail too often at NASA to be confident of it. He might get lucky.

Sambit came back a few minutes later. "The plant manager is in surgery."

"Well, fuck," Derek said, ignoring the way Sambit flinched at his cursing. The man could just get over himself. "Okay, look, if you could see what was going on inside the plant, could you shut it down?"

"In theory," Sambit said, "but we don't have the schematics."

"I'm aware of that fact," Derek snapped, "but we're wasting time here, time we don't have and time that's letting the situation get worse. We need to find the shutdown or the safety valve, whatever that looks like, and we aren't going to do it standing here."

"We can't go in there. The heat and radiation would kill us long before we found what we were looking for."

"I wasn't planning on going in there," Derek said. "I'm planning on sending Number Five in there."

"Shouldn't we call the NRC or—"

Derek ignored the other man's cautions, and walked back to the break room. He patted Fido's head a couple of times and set out a bowl of water for the dog. Then he unpacked Number Five. "Time to go to work, baby. We're going to show that ignorant asshole in the other room what we can do."

He powered up the robot and turned on the controls. There where he could see what was in front of Number Five, he didn't bother with his laptop. Later, he would connect the robot's cameras up to the laptop remotely so he could see the robot's surroundings and guide him.

"What is that?" Sambit asked when Derek guided the robot back into the room.

"This is Number Five," Derek said proudly. "You tell me where to send him, and he can go anywhere we need him to go and do anything we could do with our hands."

"That would be great if I knew where we needed him to go."

"Look, Sam," Derek said. "We could spend hours trying to find out the password for the computer. We could make phone calls and maybe get answers, or we can send Number Five exploring, make the maps as we go, and maybe find what we're looking for faster."

"Without the computers, we have no way of monitoring the system to make sure it cools down correctly. We could make matters worse."

"If we do nothing, we could both be dead. Yes, it's a risk, but it's one I think we have to take."

"You haven't the slightest idea what you're talking about."

"Maybe not," Derek said, "but it's got to be better than sitting here waiting for the core to melt down and the heat and radiation to kill us both." He opened up his laptop and activated the remote viewing and controls for Number Five. "I don't know what he's looking for so you're going to have to come help me here."

"This is a bad idea."

"Dying is a worse one."

chapter
TWO

SAMBIT scrubbed his hands over his face. His head hurt, his eyes stung from staring at the laptop screen for what seemed like hours, and his stomach was growling, when it stopped churning long enough, but they couldn't stop for food yet. Sambit's experience might be more theoretical than practical, but he knew what could happen if they didn't get the reactor under control. He'd studied Chernobyl, Three Mile Island, and Fukushima. He didn't want to add Bay City to that list with his name attached to the failure.

The man sitting next to him, with his foul mouth and brash manners, worked Sambit's last nerve, but this was the robotics engineer NASA had seen fit to send him. Not that he was all that fit for the job either. He hadn't done any practical work with nuclear reactors since he'd taken the teaching position at Texas A&M, but there hadn't been anyone else to call. Not anyone close enough to get here as fast as Sambit could. The only thing that had gone right since he'd gotten here was the little robot Marshall called Number Five. Sambit didn't claim to know anything about robotics, but he knew a useful tool when he saw one.

Number Five was definitely useful. Its track roller let it move over uneven surfaces, but Marshall had also fitted it with a lifting mechanism that allowed it to "climb" stairs. The cameras took video in three hundred sixty degrees so anyone looking at the computer screen could see everything around the robot. Its sensors detected temperature, radiation, and a score of other measurements that Sambit hadn't bothered to track because they didn't matter at the moment. Even better, the built-in GPS linked to a program on Marshall's computer that created a map as Number Five moved through the corridors. It wasn't quite as useful as the full schematics of the plant would have been, but Sambit was beginning to get a feel for the layout of the plant. It didn't match any in his eidetic memory, but he saw enough similarities to draw conclusions based on everything he'd studied.

"Turn right there."

Marshall backed Number Five up, guiding the robot with a joystick controller in one hand and another remote in the other hand with a dozen or more different buttons that told the robot to do a variety of different things. Sambit hadn't tried to figure out what. He doubted Marshall would let him anywhere near those controls anyway.

They followed the progress of Number Five down the side corridor Sambit had indicated. The robot advanced about fifteen feet according to the GPS, turning another corner only to encounter a huge pile of concrete and rebar.

"Guess we can't go that way," Marshall said, starting to turn the robot around.

"Wait!" Sambit pointed at the screen, ignoring Marshall's hand batting the finger away before it could make contact. "Can you get readings from up there near the top of the rubble?"

"I can try." Marshall fiddled with the controls, and Number Five extended an arm, stretching toward the spot Sambit had indicated. The temperature spiked nearly off the charts.

"If it's that hot back there, we've got problems. If there isn't a leak, there will be soon. We have to find the HPCI pumps and get some coolant into the reactor, or we're going to have a meltdown even with the control rods in place," Sambit said. He knew the control rods were in place. He'd been able to access that much of the data on the plant before the power shut down the first time, but while that had stopped the nuclear reaction inside the core, it wouldn't be enough to take care of the decay heat. That was where the HPCI pumps came in. Their coolant would help neutralize the stray neutrons in the core and lower the temperature and pressure enough to avert a meltdown.

"Fabulous," Marshall said, his voice dripping with sarcasm. "So tell me where to find the pumps."

"I would have said down this corridor," Sambit replied. "That's why I sent you this way in the first place."

"Number Five is good, but that's a nearly vertical climb. I'd never keep it balanced to the top, much less down the other side. And that's assuming it would survive the heat. I didn't put the kind of heat shielding on Number Five that I'd use for a robot or robotic parts we planned to use for a space mission."

The robot was, as far as Sambit could tell, Marshall's one weak spot. Any slur, however implied, about the ability of his robot resulted in immediate defensive action. "I wasn't suggesting that you should have. You asked where the pumps were. I told you where I thought they should be. There might be another access route from a different direction."

"What are we waiting for?"

Marshall spun Number Five around and directed him out to the main corridor again. "Back the way we came to check out the side halls we skipped, or forward?"

"Forward," Sambit decided after a moment's consideration. "The heat is there, which means the reactor is there. The pumps go directly into the reactor so they should be nearby too."

Marshall turned Number Five in the indicated direction. Sambit moved closer to peer over his shoulder. He caught a whiff of sweat and alcohol, a combination that usually turned his stomach, but either his stomach was too far gone from nerves and hunger to react or something was different about Marshall.

Sambit had known he was gay fairly early in high school, but in India, he had not dared tell anyone. Once he'd moved to the US, he'd gotten so used to keeping that information private that he didn't think twice about continuing that way. He'd had a few relationships, but nothing worth "coming out" for. It wasn't anyone's business anyway. Marshall clearly didn't share that opinion to judge by the rainbow bracelet around his wrist. It was his choice, of course, but it was one Sambit had never seen the sense of.

Forcing his mind back to business and away from the ill-timed shiver of awareness, Sambit focused on the screen in front of him. "Try that corridor."

Marshall turned Number Five down the corridor as indicated. The temperature rose almost immediately. "How hot can it get before it damages your robot?"

"Hotter than this," Marshall said. "I have spare parts. If I can limp it back here, even damaged, I can repair it. What am I looking for?"

"That," Sambit said, pointing to the HPCI pumps. "We have to figure out why they aren't working and get them on."

"Number Five can do what needs to be done, but you're going to have to figure out what that is because I don't know anything about this kind of pump."

Sambit nodded. "Take it around the pumps slowly so I can see what damage there might be."

Marshall directed the robot as Sambit indicated, circling the machines, zeroing in on this dial or that gauge.

"They seem to have power," Sambit said, "so the problem must be that they haven't gotten the command to turn on because the computers are down."

"Is there an On switch?" Marshall asked.

"Nothing quite that simple," Sambit said, "but we can activate them." He talked Marshall through the process of setting the pumps in motion.

"Now what?" Marshall asked when the gauges indicated that coolant was moving through the system to the core.

"Now we get the computers back online so we can see what else needs to be done," Sambit said firmly. "And don't argue with me. The HPCI pumps needed to be turned on. But now that they're working to cool and depressurize the core, we need to see what else is going on, and I can't do that remotely with a robot. I couldn't do it in person even if it were safe. I need the data from the sensors inside and around the core to know what's going on."

"Fine," Marshall said, his voice low and hard. "I'll bring Number Five back to recharge while you call around to find out what you need."

He stalked toward the door, laptop in hand, turning back as he reached the exit. "Do you want coffee?"

Sambit made a face. "No, but tea would be most welcome if there is any."

Marshall scowled again. "I'll look."

The thoughtfulness of the question, even as grudging as it had seemed, surprised Sambit. Maybe he had judged Marshall too harshly. People dealt with stress and danger differently. Maybe Marshall's surliness was a result of that rather than his usual personality. Resolving to give the man another chance, Sambit picked up the phone to call the NRC and anyone else he could think of. They needed the passwords, they needed supplies, and they needed more help.

BACK in the break room, Derek guided Number Five to the nearest plug, setting it up to recharge the robot's batteries. Once that was done, he started digging through the cabinets. Fortunately the plant had a bottled water station so he didn't have to worry about the state of the pipes, although he hoped they had some refills somewhere or they'd be thirsty soon. He ought to call Kenneth and insist they get some supplies in here, not that Kenneth was necessarily the one in charge. He was, however, the one Derek could reach.

Finding the coffee grounds, he set a pot to brew and went looking for tea for Sambit. Of course the other man would be difficult and not drink coffee like sane people. Still, Derek had offered. He was many things, but he wasn't an Indian giver—the expression amused him even though he knew Sambit was a different kind of Indian. He'd offered to make tea, so if he could find it, he'd deliver on his promise.

He finally found one lone tea bag in the back of the last cabinet. He had no idea how old it was or even if that mattered for tea, but he got hot water from the water station and put the tea bag in to steep. That done, he turned to the dog lying patiently in the corner, its ears perked up and its tail wagging. Whoever had trained the mutt had done a fantastic job. "Come here, Fido," Derek called, patting his knees.

The moment Derek called, the bundle of energy that was his dog exploded out of the corner, racing to Derek's side, his claws scraping on the linoleum floor as he skidded to a stop, tongue hanging out to one side.

"I wasn't gone that long, was I?" Derek stroked the dog's soft muzzle as he spoke, calming them both. He hadn't realized how stiff he was until he'd sat down to relax for a moment. His shoulders ached from the tension of the last hour, searching for the pumps Sambit insisted were the only way to stop the core from melting down, struggling to keep Number Five on track through the rubble and the haze. They hadn't found any bodies, thank God. He didn't know how he would've dealt with that, although he supposed they weren't out of the woods yet in that regard.

"I didn't think to bring any food for you," Derek said, scratching behind Fido's ears. "I thought I was taking you somewhere safe before I came here, but my boss apparently had a different definition of looking after you than I did. Why don't we see what's in that refrigerator? If backup power didn't go off until an hour ago like Sambit said, maybe there's stuff in there that'll still be good. You don't mind leftovers, do you?"

Fido whined and wagged his tail, so Derek opened the fridge and dug around for something he thought the dog would eat. Finding a likely-looking steak with mashed potatoes, he set the container on the ground. "I'll ask Kenneth for some proper dog food when I call him about the rest of our supplies. This'll have to do in the meantime."

Fido devoured the food in the container, returning to Derek's side as soon as he was done. He rested his chin on Derek's knee, content to be petted.

Derek closed his eyes as he sat there, trying to bring his nerves under control. Nobody in southeastern Texas had his skills with a robot. He knew that, but it didn't stop the ingrained worry that he'd screw something up, that someone else would've done a better job than he could possibly do.

"Were you able to find any tea?"

The voice startled Derek out of his wandering thoughts. He jerked upright, startling Fido, who growled unhappily. "I'm not your servant," Derek snapped. "The tea is on the counter over there. Did you reach the NRC?"

"What is with your attitude?" Sambit demanded, ignoring Derek's question. "I didn't say I expected you to bring me the tea. I simply asked if you'd found any."

"My attitude?" Derek shouted, falling back on the habit of taking the attack to his attackers that had been his only defense in junior high and high school. "What about yours? Everything by the book, all starched and prim and proper, never take any risks and shoot down anyone who tries to think outside the box? What about your attitude?"

Even in his anger, Derek could see Sambit take a deep breath, could all but see the other man make the decision not to rise to Derek's bait. "If I've offended you, I apologize. I've been on edge because of the danger we were in, but that doesn't excuse any bad behavior on my part. I will take my tea and go outside to wait for the supply caravan to arrive, along with the passwords and a few more people so we can work in shifts."

The calm in Sambit's voice and demeanor deflated Derek completely. "You don't have to do that," he said with a sigh, turning to pour his coffee so his conflicted emotions wouldn't show on his face. "I have a habit of flying off the handle, and stress makes it worse. It hasn't been a very good few days."

"For any of us," Sambit replied, his voice quiet. "If I sit here and drink my tea, will it disturb you?"

Everything about the other man disturbed Derek, but that wasn't Sambit's fault. "No."

Derek could practically feel Sambit waiting for him to finish his sentence, to invite the other man to sit down, to say something, but Derek couldn't make himself form the words. Instead, he busied himself adding creamer and sugar to his coffee until it was tan instead of black, and sweet enough to rot his teeth. He couldn't drink it any other way.

"How long before the supplies arrive?" Derek took a sip of his coffee as he turned around to face Sambit.

"They said it would be at least an hour," Sambit answered. "I asked them to bring dog food as well as food for us. I don't know how long we'll be here, but we can't stay healthy for long on vending machine snacks and soda."

"If the machines even work still," Derek agreed. "If we've got time to kill, I suppose we should figure out what kind of living quarters we'll have."

"This is it, I think," Sambit said. "They're bringing cots, they said, but we'll have to set them up wherever we can find space. The roads are washed out, and even if they weren't, we'd have to go a hundred miles or more inland to find a hotel that has power and isn't damaged. College Station is a hundred fifty miles from the coast, and we got slammed. The eye passed directly over Bay City. There's nowhere left around here."

"Well, shit," Derek said, ignoring Sambit's flinch. "I guess I'd better stake my spot out now before we get invaded by whoever they're sending to work with us." He dug in his laptop bag and pulled out his magazine, flipping through it until he found the pinups. Pulling them out carefully, he grabbed some thumbtacks from the bulletin board and used them to hang the images in one corner of the break room. "There, my own personal little sanctuary."

"Are you trying to offend people?" Sambit asked.

"Everywhere I go, I'm bombarded with images of half-dressed or naked women," Derek said. "The world assumes all men will find such things attractive. If it's all right for me to be subjected to images for their titillation, then it's fine for me to post images for mine as well."

"I'm pretty sure that constitutes sexual harassment," Sambit pointed out.

"What are they going to do?" Derek scoffed. "Fire me? Fine, I'll take Fido and go home. I do have a house and a life to go back to. Oh, and a job that actually pays me instead of this one that I'm doing out of the kindness of my heart since I can't get to Clear Lake and NASA at the moment."

"Why are you like this?" Sambit asked softly. "Why are you determined to anger everyone around you? Putting that much negative energy out into the world is sure to bring it back on you someday."

"I'm just sending back all the negative energy the world sends at me." Derek knew his voice sounded mocking, but he couldn't stop the reflexive defense mechanism he had developed after enduring years of taunts in high school for being too smart—and too gay—to fit in with the rest of his classmates. They'd taught him all too well that the best defense was a good offense, and if that meant being offensive, he could live with that. He was living on his terms, and that was all that mattered. "They take one look at this bracelet around my wrist and think they know who I am."

"And you do nothing to prove them wrong," Sambit said, indicating the pictures with a wave of his hand. "Indeed, you do everything you can to prove them right."

"What's to prove?" Derek challenged. "I'm gay. I like dick."

"As is your right," Sambit replied with that infuriating calm that made Derek want to see him flustered. "That doesn't mean you have to advertise the fact. Why does it matter if they know you're gay? It's not any of their business."

"Easy for you to say," Derek said. "I'll bet you've got a pretty little wife and five kids stashed away in College Station. You've never done anything unexpected. I know your type."

"Perhaps you do," Sambit said, "but you don't know me. You're making the same kinds of assumptions about me that you say the world makes about you. You assume I'm married because Indian men usually marry by the time they're thirty and I passed that marker a few years ago. You assume I have a family because you know Indian families are often large. For your information, I'm not married, nor have I ever been. I have no children, not even a pet. Be careful of the assumptions you make, Mr. Marshall. They say far more about you and your biases than they do about me."

Derek spluttered in indignation with absolutely no idea how to counter Sambit's argument. "Just leave me the fuck alone, okay? You don't know anything about my life."

"You are correct," Sambit said, "but I do know something about you. I know you are not a bad man. That dog adores you, and despite what you said about the time you have had him, the feeling is obviously mutual. You may hide behind your anger and bravado and bad language, but there is a gentle heart underneath it all or Fido wouldn't trust you the way he does."

"I have the food," Derek reminded Sambit, not at all comfortable with the other man's assessment of his character.

Sambit shook his head. "That's not why he follows you with his eyes the way he does. You saved him, and you've stayed by him when you could have abandoned him again. That says something far more powerful about your character than the façade you put on for the world. You should let people see that side of you too, not just show it to your dog. You might be surprised what you would receive in return."

"Nothing but heartbreak and derision," Derek replied. Sambit's words held more than a little seduction. Derek got tired sometimes of putting up the front that kept the world at a safe distance, but he'd learned the hard way not to trust anyone not related to him by blood. His parents didn't understand him, but they supported him. The rest of the world had done nothing more than knock him down and try to keep him there.

"We have a saying in my country," Sambit said with a sad smile. "Karma is a bitch, Mr. Marshall. Perhaps you should think about that."

"I don't go around doing bad things to people," Derek protested.

"Karma isn't only about action," Sambit explained. "It is about everything you put out into the world. I have only known you a few hours, but I have seen very little to foster good karma other than what you have done for your dog. It's not about what the world gives you, Mr. Marshall, but about what you put out into the world. Maybe it will give you back heartbreak and derision, as you put it, but if all you send out is that same negativity, you will miss the chance at more. Do you think Fido would have reacted the same way he did if you had come at him with your anger and cursing?"

"Leave me alone," Derek said again.

"As you wish." Sambit took his tea and left Derek alone in the break room with his pinups, his dog, and his doubts.

chapter
THREE

SAMBIT stood at the door of the power plant, sipping his tea and wishing for milk, but he had learned to drink black tea almost as a defense mechanism when he had first arrived in America. While he could usually find hot tea instead of the iced tea most Texans seemed to prefer, he rarely found milk to put in it. His colleagues who drank coffee all used the powdered creamer, which tasted like chemicals to Sambit. Black tea was better than polluting his body with that mess.

Taking another sip, Sambit thought back over his conversation with Derek. He could not decide what to make of the man. On the one hand, he was foul-mouthed, abrasive, and otherwise difficult to get along with. On the other hand, Sambit had stood and watched him with his dog for several long moments before interrupting, and the man sitting there stroking that mutt's head bore no resemblance to the angry man who had reappeared the moment Sambit spoke. Sambit had no explanation for the dichotomy, but he already recognized the fascination that came from his need to understand. In his experience, people acted predictably for the most part if one knew enough about them and their situations, and that meant Sambit still had things to discover about Derek to explain the seemingly out-of-character actions. The question was which side of Derek was the real one: the confrontational one or the one who rescued an abandoned dog and fought everyone to keep him safe after that? Sambit was inclined to believe it was the tender side because the confrontational side made sense as a façade, but the tenderness made no sense if the angry side was the sum of the man.

The image of Derek sitting in the chair, eyes closed, face defeated as he stroked the dog's head, tugged at Sambit. Nothing in that image set his teeth on edge the way Derek did the moment he opened his mouth. On the contrary, it called to Sambit's soul. His mother had always said he was a healer at heart despite his career choices. He couldn't walk by a person in pain or sorrow without trying to help. Derek might deny it—no, Derek *would* deny it—but Sambit recognized a person in need of a friend. He'd seen the images Derek hung on the wall. He wasn't at all the type Derek would find attractive, but it was better that way. They could be friends without having to worry about attraction muddying the waters. Derek wasn't Sambit's type either.

The sound of helicopters approaching drew Sambit's attention from his musings. He set aside his tea, cold now, and went out to meet them, curious to see whom the Nuclear Regulatory Commission had sent to help them.

The military pilots set the helicopters down with great precision, and the process of unloading supplies began almost before Sambit reached the landing site.

"Mr. Patel?"

"Yes, I'm Dr. Patel," Sambit replied.

"James Tucker from the NRC. I'm here to oversee the shutdown of the plant. Thank you for coming so quickly to help."

"I'm always glad to be of service," Sambit said, his hackles rising already at the implication that the project would be taken from his hands. He didn't know anything about Tucker, but he got the impression of a bureaucrat rather than an engineer. "We got the HPCI pumps running again, but without the computers or schematics, we didn't want to push our luck beyond that."

"How did you even do that?" Tucker asked. "From everything I heard in the briefing, you shouldn't have been able to get close enough to the reactor to turn them on."

"I had help," Sambit said, smothering a smile. "I'll introduce you to Derek Marshall from NASA. He'll be better equipped to explain." He could already envision Derek's reaction to the stodgy bureaucrat. This might be one instance where Derek's abrasive attitude could work in their favor. They needed the passwords the man could provide, but they didn't need the regulations that went along with them. Derek had already proven that, and after seeing Number Five at work and what Derek was capable of doing, Sambit was inclined to trust him to do it again rather than wait for more conventional means of dealing with the reactor issues. "Do you have the passwords for the central computer?"

"Yes, I brought them with me," Tucker said. "Who is Marshall? My briefing only mentioned you."

"A robotics engineer from NASA," Sambit said, escorting Tucker inside. "You did read about how they used robots to access areas of the Fukushima Dai-ichi plant in order to speed up the repairs and recovery there, didn't you? I realize that's been a few years, but someone in your position must surely keep up with advances in technology around the world."

"Of course I did," Tucker blustered, leaving Sambit with the definite impression that the man had done nothing of the kind. "I just didn't realize anyone with those skills had been brought on board here."

"I'll let him know you're here while you're getting the computers up and running," Sambit said. "He'll be eager to get back to work."

"We'll have to take stock of the situation and see what needs to be done and—"

"Mr. Tucker," Sambit interrupted. He'd heard all the same arguments coming from his own mouth when he was talking to Derek, but the man had changed his mind. "Not to put too fine a point on it, but time is of the essence here. Get the computers online and then get out of the way so Mr. Marshall and I can do what needs to be done."

"Hey!" one of the supply personnel shouted. "What am I supposed to do with this dog food?"

"I'll take it," Sambit said, leaving Tucker to make his own way inside. "I know a very hungry pup who will be very happy to see it." He took the huge bag from the soldier, who looked about fifteen and scared out of his mind. "Don't worry," he said. "There's not enough radiation out here to hurt you."

"It's not that," the soldier admitted. "I've never seen anything like what we flew over to get here. There's nothing left."

"Not right now," Sambit agreed, "but people will come back and rebuild. We'll get the power back on here. The utility companies will get the lines restrung, and the people will come back. It'll just take time."

"I hope so," the soldier said. "Thank you for what you're doing here."

Sambit shook his head. "I'm just doing my part."

Hefting the dog food, he went back inside, leaving the soldiers to finish unloading the supplies. The new additions to the crew could help carry supplies in as well. He had more important things to do, like making friends with the man he had just decided would be his partner for the rest of the time they were here. "Derek?" Sambit called, walking into the break room. "I have Fido's food."

"The supplies arrived?"

"They're outside unloading," Sambit said, setting the carton down. "Why don't you feed Fido first, and then we can go see what the suit from the NRC has managed to get done on the computers. I can tell already he's going to be a pain."

"I thought you wanted help from the NRC," Derek said.

Sambit chuckled. "No, I wanted the passwords from the NRC. We proved what we could do earlier today. I don't need any more convincing."

"Well, color me surprised," Derek said. He opened the bag of dog food and poured some out for Fido, petting the dog's head as he encouraged the dog to eat. Sambit stroked the silky ears as well.

"Is Number Five ready for another trip into the reactor?" Sambit asked.

"It should be close to fully recharged by now," Derek replied. "We only used an hour or so of its battery life. How big of a pain in the ass is this suit going to be?"

"I'm sure you can handle him," Sambit said, quite confident Tucker would be no match for Derek's sarcastic wit. "At the moment, nobody knows what's going on in the plant as well as we do, so we have that in our favor, and we also know where the problem spots are as far as blocked corridors, and since we have the earlier readings, we can see if there's been any change if we go back to an area we went through before. I'm not sure even the plant manager could do more right now than we can. Tucker certainly can't."

"What else do we need to do?" Derek asked as he unplugged Number Five and guided the robot toward the door.

"It'll depend on what we find when we look at the computers," Sambit said. "It could be the HPCI pumps did their job and all we'll need to do is examine the reactor vessel and primary containment system to make sure they weren't damaged by the storm. Or it could be we'll still have heat and pressure issues in the core, at which point we'll have to make some repairs, although we might be able to do some of that remotely if the systems are functioning."

"I'll leave that to you," Derek said. "You tell me where to send my robot, and I'll get it there."

"I know you will," Sambit said as they headed back to the main bank of computers. Sambit saw the look of surprise on Derek's face, but now wasn't the time to explain the realizations he'd had while waiting for the supply convoy. If they had time later, they could talk, and if not, that was fine too. Actions would do far more to win Derek's confidence than words. Derek had obviously heard far too many meaningless words in his life.

THE moment Derek laid eyes on Tucker, he understood Sambit's antipathy. Everything about the man was officious, from his suit to the supercilious expression on his face. That would have been bad enough. The way Tucker dismissed him completely, speaking only to Sambit, was the nail in the other man's coffin as far as Derek was concerned.

"Mr. Patel, what is that?"

"It's Dr. Patel," Derek replied before Sambit could reply, "and 'that' is my robot. The robot that is going to save our collective asses, so get out of the way and let Dr. Patel tell me where to send him and what to do with him."

Tucker sputtered and fumed, but Derek pushed past him, gesturing for Sambit to take a seat at the computer.

Sambit moved past the NRC representative with more grace and less aggression, but Derek could see the approval in his smirk as he sat down and began to study the display of readings on the monitor.

"We need to go back to where we had the big blockage," Sambit told Derek. "I'm getting inconsistent temperature readings from the core. We need to see what the situation really is, and that's where we had the highest temperature readings before."

"On it," Derek said, sending Number Five rolling out of the room and back toward the blocked corridor. Behind him, Tucker demanded explanations, but Derek ignored him. He couldn't give them anyway— that was Sambit's area of expertise—and he had more important things to focus on, like making sure Number Five went where he was supposed to as smoothly and efficiently as possible.

Sambit apparently had somewhat more patience with Tucker than Derek did, because he heard the softly accented voice begin a detailed explanation that went right over Derek's head. It didn't matter. He didn't need to understand the physics of nuclear reactions to guide his robot where it needed to go.

"Dr. Patel," he interrupted when Number Five was in place, "I have new readings for you."

Sambit joined him at his laptop immediately, breaking off the conversation with Tucker. His hand rested on Derek's shoulder as he bent over to look at the temperature indicator on the laptop screen. Derek suppressed a totally inappropriate shiver as his body reacted.

"It's cooler than it was," Sambit said, "but still elevated. I wish we knew what was behind that mess."

"The Standby Gas Treatment system."

Derek and Sambit both turned to see who had spoken. A tall black woman joined them at the computer. "Lyrica Johnson," she added by way of introduction. "I'm the night shift manager. I was evacuated, but when I heard about the problems, I got in touch with the NRC and they flew me in."

"Should it be this hot back there?" Sambit asked, showing her the readings.

"No, that's not normal. Can you get a camera up there so we can see what's going on?"

"It's a nearly vertical climb," Derek said for the second time that day. "Number Five can climb steps, but it can't defy the laws of gravity. Is there another way in?"

"Not usually, but all that concrete came from somewhere. If it left an exterior hole, we could maybe go in that way," Lyrica said.

"We need a second robot," Sambit said. "One to go outside and look for that while Number Five works inside. Derek, let's check the gauges on the HPCI pumps. We can't do anything about this right now so we need to see what's going on in the core as much as we can."

Derek nodded and sent Number Five to the area where they had found the pumps earlier. They were all still working, although the pressure gauges continued to show high levels of pressure inside the core. "It's not cooling down fast enough," Sambit muttered.

"Did you add boron to the coolant?" Lyrica asked.

Sambit shook his head. "We didn't even have power when we got here. Getting the generators online and the pumps working again were our first priorities."

"As they should have been. Okay, Derek, is it?" Derek nodded. "What can that gadget of yours do?"

"Anything you want it to," Derek said, "except climb straight up and survive an explosion. It has some heat shielding, but not extensive since it's a prototype. I can add that kind of shielding, but it will decrease the mobility."

"I've got containers of boron that need to be added to the coolant mix," Lyrica said, "and the radiation readings from your little friend there suggest it wouldn't be safe for us to do it manually."

Derek looked at Sambit for confirmation. He liked Lyrica's no-nonsense attitude, but he didn't know her well enough to trust her. For some reason, though, he trusted Sambit. Sambit nodded.

"Tell me where they are."

"What about the depressurization system?" Sambit asked before Lyrica could reply. "Is it worth trying to let a little pressure out now to buy us time to get the boron solution into the core?"

"That's against protocol!" Tucker protested. "We have no idea what kind of radiation levels are inside the core at the moment, and if the secondary containment structure is compromised, you could be releasing dangerous levels of radiation into the air."

"Shut up, Tucker," Derek said. "They're professionals. They know the risks."

"The risk is minimal," Lyrica said. "The vents open into the wetwell. It might be flooded, but it's underground so it shouldn't have been damaged by the tornado or hurricane winds. It's certainly less of a risk than a core meltdown or breach would be."

"Tell me where to go," Derek said, turning his back on Turner.

Lyrica gave him directions to the ADS override, not even bothering to see if the computerized system would work. Derek followed her instructions to the letter.

"It's working," Sambit said from the main computer station. "The pressure is going down in the core."

"Good," Lyrica said. "Let's leave it for another minute, and then we'll turn it back off. We don't know the condition of the wetwell, and until we do, we shouldn't put too much stress on the system."

They waited out the allotted time, and Derek guided Number Five to shut the valves again.

"This is all highly unusual," Tucker said again.

"Mr. Tucker," Sambit said from the computer, "it occurs to me that we've all focused on this reactor because we knew it was damaged, but no one has checked on units one and two. Perhaps you should take a couple of people and make sure they shut down correctly and that the backup systems are dealing with the decay heat appropriately. It would be a shame to work so hard over here only to have a disaster over there because we didn't realize there was a problem."

Tucker blanched and bustled out of the room, calling names for people to accompany him.

"Thank God," Lyrica said when Tucker was out of earshot. "Now if we can just keep him out of our hair."

"I knew there was a reason I liked you," Derek said. "Sam, I think she's okay."

"Sambit," Sambit corrected, but his smile was indulgent. "Welcome to the team, Lyrica."

"I think I'm the one who should be welcoming you," Lyrica countered, "but either way, it's good to work with people who can think on their feet. Okay, let's get the boron in the coolant and see where we are. I don't suppose you have a second one of those robots stashed away somewhere?"

"No," Derek said. "It's a prototype. I plan to patent it eventually, but I'm not done tweaking it yet."

"Damn. Well, I guess we'll just have to make do with one, then."

"If we have another robot of any kind, I can make adjustments to it," Derek offered. "That's what I do at NASA. Take other people's robots and make them do what NASA needs them to do instead of what they were designed to do."

"Which would be faster?" Sambit asked. "Tweaking an existing robot or building another one like Number Five?"

"With the right parts, it's just as easy to build a new one from scratch," Derek replied, "because part of tweaking an existing robot is working on its programming and interface with the controls, and that's what takes the longest. If I simply install my programming to begin with, that could save hours of work."

"Then we'll have to persuade Tucker to get you the parts you need," Lyrica declared.

"And make sure there's someone else who can operate it," Sambit added. "I've watched him with those controls. It's not just something you pick up and can immediately do. They brought Derek here for more reasons than one."

The comment surprised Derek. He hadn't realized Sambit thought so highly of him. Derek certainly hadn't given him any reason to. Silently he resolved to be nicer to the other man. He'd need an ally against Tucker if he had any hope of saving his sanity. "I brought some parts with me, more as replacement parts for Number Five than to build a second robot, but it's a start, although the time I take to construct a second robot is time I'm not operating the first one. Once the second one is built, I can teach someone how to operate it even if they can't maintain it," Derek said. "It takes practice, like anything else, but it's a lot like playing video games. Once you get the hang of it, it's not so hard."

"Tell that to someone who's good at video games," Sambit said with a short laugh. "I'll leave the operating to you and concentrate on figuring out what needs to be done."

chapter
FOUR

IT TOOK another hour to transfer enough boron into the coolant to satisfy Lyrica and Sambit, and by then, Derek's stomach was demanding food.

"Break time," he declared when they didn't immediately assign him another task. "I fed Fido, but I haven't eaten since this morning."

"Fido?" Lyrica asked.

"His dog," Sambit explained, standing and stretching, the arch of his back drawing Derek's attention to his body. Derek swallowed hard. *Not my type*, he told himself firmly. *So not my type.* That didn't stop his eyes from lingering as Sambit bent forward, touching his toes and highlighting his ass.

"I rescued him from the house down the street," Derek said, forcing his eyes away from Sambit and toward Lyrica. "I couldn't turn around and leave him again, and there wasn't exactly time to find a place for him."

"So you brought him with you?" Lyrica asked, her eyes bright with amusement. "Oh, that'll make Tucker's day. Well done, Derek."

Derek and Sambit both chuckled.

"Wait until Tucker sees Derek's other additions to the break room," Sambit added. "He'll never recover."

"Oh?" Lyrica said. "Do tell."

Derek shrugged. "I just hung a couple of pictures on the wall. We're going to be living here so I wanted to make it feel a little more like home."

Sambit snorted. "So your room at home is decorated with pinups too?"

Lyrica rolled her eyes. "What is it with men and their fascination with tits?"

"I wouldn't know," Sambit replied primly, making Derek do a double take as he wondered exactly how to interpret that, "and neither would Derek." He grabbed Derek's arm and pulled his sleeve back to reveal the rainbow bracelet.

Lyrica's face brightened. "Now that's the kind of pinup I can appreciate!"

"I'm sure Tucker won't," Sambit said.

"Tucker can go stuff himself," Lyrica said, looping one arm through Derek's and the other through Sambit's. "In the absence of the regular plant manager, I'm the senior employee here. He can write all the reports he wants. We're the ones running this show."

They walked back into the break room. Three other people, two men and another woman, milled about, unpacking supplies, spreading out army issue cots and blankets, and generally making far more noise than necessary as far as Derek was concerned.

"Come here, Fido," he called, seeing the dog cowering in the corner. Immediately the dog bounded over to him. "Do you want to go outside, boy?"

"Don't go out without a Geiger counter and dosimeter," Sambit said immediately. "The control area is shielded so we shouldn't get high levels of radiation here unless that's damaged, but we have no idea what the conditions outside are."

"I get that, but the dog has to have a break, and I don't figure people want him shitting in the corner," Derek said. "So unless you have a better suggestion, we're going outside."

"Stay as close to the building as possible," Lyrica said. "It should provide some protection from radiation even outside, and come back inside as soon as he's done. If he needs exercise, we'll have to make sure he gets it inside until we're sure we don't have a radiation leak outside. We'll see about some dinner while you're taking care of your dog. Is there anything you don't eat?"

"Nope, omnivore here," Derek said. "Okay, Fido, let's go outside, but stay close to me, all right? I don't have a leash for you, and I don't want you running off and getting lost or hurt."

He had no idea if the dog could understand him, but it trotted along next to him as he walked toward the exit. He stayed in the doorway while Fido sniffed around a little, picking his way over the flooded grass. He stopped and did his business before running back to Derek's side. "Good boy. Let's go back inside."

When they'd returned to the break room, Fido curled up in his corner again. Derek took one of the cots and moved it over to the same corner, giving Fido somewhere to hide if he wanted.

"There you go," Derek said, bending down and patting Fido's head. "You can keep an eye on my bag and my boys. How does that sound?"

Fido closed his eyes and leaned into Derek's hand. Derek smiled. He'd never wanted a dog, but now that he had one, he wondered why he'd resisted. He could get used to true unconditional affection.

"Are you the one who hung those up?" one of the other men whom Derek had not yet met asked.

"Yes," Derek said. "What of it? There's nothing wrong with a bare chest."

The man's lips curled, but before he could say anything, Lyrica was at Derek's side. "Nothing wrong at all," she agreed, "although I wouldn't complain if the jeans on that one cowboy slid a little lower down. He's something else."

"He is," Derek agreed. "That's William Jones. He's a favorite of mine."

The man who'd asked about the pictures made a sound of disgust and walked away. "Don't mind Jeremiah," she said softly. "He's a born-again Christian who thinks he has the market cornered on righteousness. He's a pain, but he's a hard worker and he knows his way around the systems here."

"Great," Derek said, "a Bible thumper. Just what I need."

"Sarcasm becomes you," Lyrica teased. "You, Sambit, and I will be one team. We'll put him on the other team so you don't have to deal with him."

"So who are the other two?" Derek asked.

"Melanie Bowman and Thomas Dougherty, two other plant employees," Lyrica replied. "They may not have your skills with a robot, but they can at least monitor systems during our off shift, even if they can't do as much to fix problems as we can."

"If one of them is willing to learn from a fag, I can show them how to use the robot," Derek said, unable to stop the bitterness in his voice.

"Don't judge us all by Jeremiah," Lyrica said. "Bay City might not be Houston, but that doesn't mean we're all redneck hicks with nothing better to do than bash the gay guy."

"Sorry," Derek said. He was even mostly sincere. Lyrica had been nothing but kind to him since she'd arrived, and he had no real reason to assume Melanie and Thomas would be any different. One bad apple didn't ruin the whole bag, as his mother was fond of saying.

"Soup's ready," Sambit said, handing Derek a bowl. "It's nothing fancy, but they didn't bring us anything fancy. Still, it's hot, and hopefully it'll be filling."

Derek looked down at the beef and vegetable soup. Definitely not fancy. "We did survive a hurricane," he said, trying to lighten the suddenly heavy mood. "I suppose we should be thankful for hurricane rations. It's not like we have a gourmet kitchen at our disposal anyway, right?"

"No, just a microwave and a coffee maker," Lyrica said. "We'll make do with that until we can get something better or until we can get out of here."

"So how long are we likely to be stuck here?" Derek asked, taking a sip of the soup. "Best and worst case scenarios."

"Worst case scenario is something like Chernobyl or Fukushima," Sambit said, "where repairs really aren't an option, and we have to seal the plant and abandon it permanently. That's the last resort, especially here because of the other two reactors. Unless Tucker finds something, there's no reason they couldn't be reactivated as soon as there's a crew to monitor them."

"Best case scenario, a couple of days," Lyrica continued. "We cool the core down, check all the containment systems, and leave it to restart once it's declared safe to be back in the area post-hurricane."

"And likeliest scenario?" Derek asked.

"Somewhere in between," Sambit said. Lyrica nodded in agreement. "The systems are damaged enough that the computer readings aren't accurate, which means we can't just turn everything back on and assume the automated systems will work properly. Not that we'd ever do that with a nuclear power plant, but we already know the automated systems are compromised. We have to determine the extent of the damage to the core and containment vessels first, then to the monitoring systems, and get those repaired or new systems in place. Granted, not all of that has to happen immediately, and not all of that will require your assistance, especially if the radiation and heat are under control so that it's safe for people to move about the complex, but this isn't going to be over tomorrow."

"Then I guess the next thing to do is to see what kind of damage there is outside," Derek said.

"There are hazmat suits, although we'd have to see what sizes we can find," Lyrica said. "They're only good for about fifteen minutes because of the size of the breathing apparatus, but we could see quite a bit in fifteen minutes, and we can always come back inside and switch suits if we haven't seen everything we need to see."

"We can also send Number Five," Derek suggested. "I'm happy to tramp around in a hazmat suit if that will be the most help, but the drizzle had stopped when Fido and I went outside. Number Five can deal with a certain amount of moisture in the air and on his track roller, and while radiation can eventually damage the circuits, it's not as sensitive as we are."

"We'll keep that in mind," Lyrica said, "but some things are just best seen in person, and I think this may be one of those times. I don't know how else to explain it except to say that there's a sense of a situation that goes along with being in the middle of it that nothing else can replace."

Derek had spent his career thus far creating machines that provided that sense of situation across the gaps of outer space, but he didn't argue. In this case, they could go out into the middle of the situation and have that personal touch, so he saw no reason to insist.

Fido whined when Derek got up and started out of the room again. "I know, boy," he said, going back to reassure the dog. "You don't know what's going on, you're in a strange place, and the one person you do know keeps disappearing on you. You're doing great. It'll be someone else's shift soon, and then I can sit here and keep you company, okay?"

"I'll watch him if it will help."

Derek looked up to see the woman Lyrica had identified as Melanie. "I don't know how he feels about strangers," Derek began, only to realize how inane a statement that was when he had been a stranger to the dog only that morning. "But if you're sure you don't mind, I'd worry less knowing he wasn't left alone again."

"Again?" Melanie asked.

Derek explained quickly how he'd found Fido that morning.

"That's horrible!"

Derek decided he liked her. "Stay with Melanie, Fido, okay? I'll be back soon." Fido wagged his tail and moved to Melanie's side. "Good boy," Derek praised before joining Lyrica and Sambit in the hallway. "Let's get this done. It's getting late. We don't have a lot of daylight left."

They sorted through the hazmat suits in storage until they found ones that would fit well enough to protect them. Lyrica helped them get the suits on and fitted correctly and showed them how to switch on the two-way radios that would let them communicate while they were outside.

"I may as well be wearing a spacesuit," Derek said as they clunked toward the door, the steel-toed boots feeling awkwardly heavy compared to the weight of the light boots he'd had on earlier.

"Pretty much," Lyrica agreed through the radio. "These suits are designed for situations where everything out there is presumed to be bad. The only thing it doesn't have is temperature control."

"So what are we looking for?" Sambit asked as they tramped across the flooded yard toward the side of the control building.

"Anything that isn't as it should be," Lyrica said.

"That might help Sam, but it doesn't help me much," Derek said, turning his head left and right as much as the hazmat suit would allow to try to get a feel for the area.

"So think of it as a chance to get the lay of the land for later, when you have to do this with Number Five," Sambit suggested, "and some things will be obvious even to a layman's eyes."

Derek rounded a corner and caught sight of a body on the ground, the legs caught beneath fallen concrete. "Like that?" he said with a grimace.

"Oh, God," Lyrica said, the words as much a prayer as a curse. She hurried to the body. Derek and Sambit followed, lifting the concrete slab and pulling the body free.

"I almost don't want to turn him over," Lyrica said. "It's almost certainly someone I know, and I'm not sure I want to know who."

"If you would rather go inside, Derek and I can take care of him," Sambit offered, his voice so rich with compassion that Derek found himself nodding his agreement even though he had no interest in dealing with a dead body.

"No," Lyrica said, "I'm the manager. I need to deal with this."

"You don't have to," Derek said, echoing Sambit's offer.

"I appreciate the thoughtfulness," Lyrica said, "but I'll have to deal with it eventually. I'll have to fill out the paperwork if nothing else. It was a job site accident that killed him."

"It was a hurricane that killed him," Derek said, bending as best he could and helping Sambit roll the body over so Lyrica could see the man's face. Derek was glad of the heavy suit that blocked what had to be an awful smell emanating from the bloated form. He could see early signs of decay already, suggesting the man, whoever he was, had been here a couple of days at least. Derek was no expert, but he'd watched enough forensics shows to know that decomposition didn't start instantly. "Do you know him?" he asked when Lyrica didn't say anything.

"Yes," she replied. "That's Ernesto Diaz, the second shift manager. I took over from him every night when I came on night shift. We weren't friends, but we were friendly."

"Is there somewhere we can take him?" Derek asked. "Somewhere inside at least until the coroner or someone can get here."

"That could be weeks," Lyrica said, her voice breaking.

"All the more reason to move him inside where his body is protected from the elements and any scavengers who survived the storm," Sambit said. "Even a storage shed would be better than leaving him outside."

"We can put him in with the used rods, I guess." Lyrica pointed to a shed on the far side of the complex. "It's not an area we'll need to access until the plants are running again, and even then not right away."

"Stay here. Sambit and I will take care of him."

"You'll need my access code," Lyrica said, "and I should come. I need to do right by him."

Derek let it go, bending awkwardly to pick up the man's shoulders. Sambit lifted his legs, and together they crossed the waterlogged yard to the shed Lyrica had indicated. She entered her code in the keypad, which, mercifully, still worked and opened the door to let them inside. They carried the body over the sill, laying it out along the wall. Derek crossed himself as Sambit knelt and whispered a prayer in a language Derek didn't understand.

"Thank you," Lyrica said to both of them. "Now we have about seven minutes left on our air supply. As important as it was to take care of Ernesto, we need to check out the reactor."

After making sure the door locked behind them, Lyrica led them toward the core for unit three. "Keep an eye on your Geiger counter," Sambit told Derek. "We're fine inside the suits, but a spike in radiation will let us know if there's a problem."

They circled the containment building until they found the hole Lyrica had postulated must be there. Almost immediately, Derek's Geiger counter started sounding. "Not good, guys."

"I see that," Lyrica said. "We've got to get closer anyway. Until I see what's going on, I won't know what the problem is or how to fix it. We've got three minutes left."

"Will the suits protect us against this level of radiation?"

"Not for long, but for long enough for me to check out the Standby Gas Treatment installation. Stay here."

Derek met Sambit's eyes through the glazed plastic of their masks. Of one accord they followed her over the collapsed concrete and into the corridor they hadn't been able to explore before. Sweat ran down Derek's back as the heat mounted, but they dodged downed rebar and caught up with Lyrica. "I thought I said to stay there."

"You already know we don't follow directions well," Derek replied. "Tell us what we're looking for so we can get the fuck out of here. I'm sweating like a stuck pig inside this contraption."

"That," Lyrica said, pointing to the Standby Gas Treatment system. "It's supposed to filter air so it's safe to be released into the environment, but with this hole in the containment wall, it's useless. We've got to get back inside. We're going to run out of air."

She led them back toward the entrance to the control building at a half-run, all they could manage in the bulky protective gear. At the entrance, she unfastened the hood and pulled it back. Sweat and maybe tears covered her face. Sambit followed his example, peeling back his hood and starting to take off the hazmat suit. Sweat had pooled under his arms, soaking his shirt. He took it off as well, so he stood in only a sleeveless undershirt, the ribbed fabric clinging to every dip of muscle. Derek swallowed hard as he unfastened his own helmet. He hadn't had any hint that Sambit was hiding a body like *that* underneath his buttoned-up exterior.

"Get rid of the suit," Lyrica said. "You can't wear it inside now that it's been exposed to that level of radiation. We'll leave them out here for now and deal with them properly when we have the means."

Derek stripped the hazmat suit the rest of the way off, relieved to have one less layer of gear on in the stifling humidity of a late summer day in south Texas. The temperature hadn't risen too high yet, fortunately, but that just meant they were breathing cool water instead of hot water. At least the climate control in the building seemed to be working at the moment. If it went out, they'd really be miserable.

"Johnson, Patel, Marshall, what do you think you were doing, going outside without my approval?" Tucker shouted the minute they stepped back inside.

"Pissing you off," Derek replied flippantly. "Dr. Patel, Dr. Johnson, I believe we're off duty. We'll see you in about twelve hours, Tucker. In the meantime, try not to make matters worse, will you?"

He walked into the break room and flopped down on his cot, sweaty clothes and all. Fido crawled out from under his cot immediately, whining as he rested his head on Derek's arm. Derek patted his head absently.

"Mr. Marshall," Tucker said, coming into the break room, "we need to have a word about your attitude."

"No, we don't," Derek replied, not even opening his eyes. "I don't work for the power plant, the Nuclear Regulatory Commission, or any other organization that gives you any authority in my regard. If you'd care to take it up with NASA, you can contact Kenneth Woodall. If *he* has an issue with my attitude, then I'll worry about it. Until then, go away and leave me alone. I'd like to get some sleep so I'll be ready to do whatever Dr. Johnson and Dr. Patel need me to do tomorrow."

Derek could hear Tucker spluttering in frustration, but he didn't acknowledge the man any further. He'd played nice all day—well, nice for him anyway—and he was done.

"You don't gain anything by antagonizing him, you know."

The words were accompanied by a nudge to his ankle and a sudden dip in the cot. That brought Derek's eyes open to the vision of Sambit perched on the end of his cot, still in his undershirt and dress slacks. He'd wiped the sweat from his face and chest, but a drip still lingered on the end of his hair. Derek fought the irrational need to sit up and brush it away.

"I gain a hell of a lot of satisfaction," Derek said. He didn't reach for that tempting bead of sweat, but he did sit up. He felt far too vulnerable lying flat on his bed beneath Sambit's piercing gaze.

"He isn't going away just because he's a pain," Sambit said. "The more you antagonize him, the harder it will be for all of us to work with him. You get to go back to NASA eventually, but Lyrica would like to keep working here. I'm in the classroom rather than in a plant, but I still work in this field. He could make our lives difficult even if he can't do anything to yours once you leave."

"I'll get you a job at NASA," Derek offered. "We've been experimenting with using nuclear power on some of the long-range spacecraft. You could consult on those projects."

"That's a generous offer, but is it really one you can make?" Sambit said. "Just think a little about the rest of us before you make too much of an enemy of him. Unless you're trying to make an enemy of the rest of us as well?"

"No, of course not," Derek said.

Sambit cocked an eyebrow at him.

"Okay, fine, I'm not Mr. Congeniality, and I was a little abrasive when we first met, but it's been a rough few days. Yes, I know"—he waved his hand to cut off Sambit's interruption—"it's been a rough few days for everyone. I get that. Really, I do, but that's the best I've got at the moment, okay? I walked out of my house this morning to find barely half a dozen houses in my neighborhood still standing. I found Fido in the wreckage down the street, soaking wet and shaking from fear. It's a miracle he didn't drown or get crushed when the building fell down around him. I got a series of nasty phone calls from my boss, and then orders to pack up my robot and come here where I know no one, know nothing about what I'm supposed to be doing to help, and where the risk to my long-term health is as great or greater than that bitch of a storm. I'm entitled to feel a little rough around the edges."

"You waited out the storm at home?"

Derek shrugged. "Do you know how many times I've seen people evacuate because this was 'the big one'?" Sambit shook his head. "I don't either. I've lost count, it's happened so often. The storms fizzle out or they change direction or they don't do the damage everyone says they will, so I shrugged and figured this one would be the same as all the rest."

"Only it wasn't."

"No, it certainly wasn't," Derek agreed, "but by the time I realized it wasn't, it was too late to try to get out. My house is on a bit of a rise so it didn't flood, and I have storm shutters so it was safe from flying debris, but on my motorcycle, I'd have been toast."

"You were lucky."

"I was beyond lucky, and I know it, but it's left me a little shaken."

Sambit nodded. "If you won't be offended by the suggestion, I know something that might help."

"I already tried tequila," Derek joked. "It didn't work."

Sambit smiled. "No, not alcohol. Yoga."

"Yoga?" Derek repeated. "How is that supposed to help?"

"Stand up and take off your socks and I'll show you," Sambit offered.

Derek was skeptical, but he didn't have anything better to do with his time. Fido stood up as soon as he did, but Derek patted the dog's head and told him to go lie down. He curled up under Derek's cot, eyes fixed on Derek as he pulled off his socks.

"Okay, convince me."

Sambit stood up straight, feet together, palms against each other in front of his chest, and took a deep breath. Derek mimicked the pose awkwardly.

"Just relax and breathe for a moment," Sambit said, his eyes closing. Derek tried to relax and breathe, but the sounds of people moving around in the hallway distracted him.

"Don't pay attention to them," Sambit said without opening his eyes. "Concentrate inward. All that matters is your breath."

"How did you know I was paying attention to them?" Derek asked. "You didn't even look at me."

"I can hear your breathing," Sambit said, "and it isn't calm and even yet, which means you're thinking about something other than that. You can close the door if it will help."

Derek closed the door, suddenly aware of Sambit's proximity as he returned to his spot. He told himself to stop being ridiculous. He didn't know if Sambit was gay, and even if he was, the professor was *so* not Derek's type. Except that he had a sharp wit to go with his education, a toned body to go with his conservative clothes, and patience with Derek's foibles. It was a deadly combination. Then Sambit arched his back, lifting his hands at the same time before exhaling audibly and bending forward to touch his toes. Derek swore Sambit's body simply folded in half at his hips.

Fuck.

He had to find out if Sambit was gay without giving away his interest.

"So what do I do now?" He needed Sambit to stand back up or he wouldn't be responsible for his actions.

Sambit stood up and returned to the same position as before. "Start at the beginning. It's the end of the day, not the beginning, but the Salute to the Sun is still a good way to relax and invigorate your body and mind."

"Is that what you were doing?"

"That was the first part of it, yes," Sambit said. "Take a deep breath, lift your hands, and lean back as far as you can without losing your balance."

Derek did as Sambit said, feeling the stretch along his abdomen as he arched his back. He couldn't go back nearly as far as Sambit did, but he had already realized this was one field on which he couldn't compete with the other man.

"Now exhale as you bend forward and touch your toes."

Derek's mind skittered back to the image of Sambit bent double. He kept his breathing steady, trying to focus on the yoga rather than on his instructor. He bent forward, groaning at the stretch down the backs of his legs. To his dismay, he couldn't even touch his toes without bending his knees.

"Right leg back into a lunge," Sambit directed, moving in time with his words. Derek imitated Sambit's stance. "Now the other leg, into a plank."

About the time his shoulders started burning from holding the pushup position, Derek gave up watching Sambit and concentrated on breathing and not making a fool of himself. He pushed his hips up into the position Sambit called Down Dog, pulled his leg forward for another lunge, returned to the toe touch position, and stood, arching his back again before returning to the prayer position where they'd started. "Holy fuck. That hurts."

"You are stiff," Sambit said. "That's why. It should feel good, energizing, not painful."

"I obviously need more practice, then," Derek said, slumping back onto his cot.

"Then we should practice," Sambit insisted. "Up. Two minutes is not enough to help your state of mind or your state of body. We will do it four more times, and then we'll decide what to do next."

"Can't I just go for a run?" Derek asked.

"Where?" Sambit countered. "You can't go outside because of the radiation, and we don't know that the rest of this building is any safer. You can do this right here without any extra space or equipment. It might not be ideal, but I assure you I can arrange as hard a workout for you as you would like."

"I believe it," Derek said, levering himself off the cot again. "All right. Fifteen minutes. We'll do fifteen minutes of yoga and we'll see how I feel then."

"Half an hour would be better," Sambit said. "You wouldn't go for a fifteen-minute run."

"I would if I'd never been a runner before and didn't have any stamina," Derek said. "Just remember I've never done this before."

"I'll take it easy on you," Sambit promised, "as long as you don't take it easy on yourself."

"What does that mean?"

"It means that it's possible to go through the motions in yoga without investing yourself in it," Sambit explained. "Or you can do something simple like the Salute to the Sun with great concentration and effort and get a good workout in a few minutes. Yoga is as much about your mind as it is about your body."

"So you'll agree to do poses that are relatively uncomplicated if I promise to concentrate on doing them right?" Derek verified.

"Exactly."

They did four more repetitions of the Salute to the Sun Sambit had started with. By the time that was done, Derek was breathing hard, the muscles in his legs protesting the unfamiliar exercise.

"Five more minutes," Derek reminded Sambit.

"We will concentrate on balance, then," Sambit said. "The poses are not hard. Holding them requires great focus, and that is what will take your mind off everything that has brought negative energy into your life in the past few days."

Derek was skeptical, but he lifted one foot in imitation of Sambit's pose, resting it on the inside of his other knee as he lifted his hands above his head and tried to keep his balance.

"Find a place on the other wall, a vertical line works best, and look only at that," Sambit directed. "Nothing exists but that one spot."

Derek focused on the edge of the soda machine and found that his body suddenly felt steadier. "How the hell does that work?" he asked.

"Concentrate," Sambit replied simply. "Hold that pose."

Derek looked back to the soda machine and concentrated.

"Now switch legs."

That side wasn't nearly as easy, even with the vertical line. Derek had to put his foot down several times to keep from falling.

"Don't worry so much," Sambit said, his foot coming gracefully back to the ground. "Everyone has a stability side and a mobility side. You will always balance better on one side than the other, but that will improve with time and practice."

"You say that like I'm going to do this with you again," Derek said, sitting down on his cot again.

"You will." Sambit's voice was so confident Derek almost refused just to annoy him, but when he took a deep breath and took stock of his body, he realized he was more relaxed than he'd been before. Sore from stretching so much, but more relaxed.

"Maybe. We'll see how tomorrow goes."

chapter
FIVE

SAMBIT left Derek alone after their shared yoga time. As much as he would have liked to linger, Sambit could tell Derek needed a break. The thought amused him because he'd only known the other man for a few hours, but even with the yoga practice, tension rolled off Derek in waves, far more so than when he'd first arrived. Out in the hall, Sambit moved through a few more advanced poses, letting the familiar movements stretch his muscles and ease his own troubled thoughts.

Finding the body of the second shift manager had shaken him. While not as strict as many Hindus about the caste system, he had grown up with a distinct aversion to dead bodies as unclean. To Lyrica, though, the body hadn't been unclean. It had been a friend who deserved a better end than lying facedown in the mud and being left to rot. Sambit consoled himself that the hazmat suit had protected him from everything else. It could protect him from contact with a dead body as well. That had been bad enough, but the readings on the Geiger counters as they climbed around the core containment buildings were far more troubling in the long term. That level of radiation could kill them—and render large portions of the surrounding areas unusable—if they couldn't get them under control.

And then there was Derek. Foul-mouthed, prickly Derek, who had adopted a stray dog and now defended that dog with all his considerable temper. Defensive, combative Derek who had insisted on going outside with Lyrica and Sambit even though it was so far beyond his area of expertise that he could have used that as an excuse to stay where it was safe. Out-and-proud Derek.

That was the hardest part for Sambit to understand. He had never felt the need to share his sexuality with anyone other than his lovers, not that he'd had all that many. His family had given up on arranging a marriage for him after he'd repeatedly refused to meet the girls they'd picked out, but that was a matter of principle. Whether he stayed with a lover for a few weeks or for the rest of his life, he intended to pick that person, not have his parents make the decision for him. He'd told them that in no uncertain terms. He'd simply neglected to mention the preferred gender of those lovers. He had a hard and fast rule about mixing business and pleasure, so he'd never dated anyone at work, which meant his colleagues didn't know he was gay, but they didn't need to. When they had gatherings away from work, they always invited him and a guest, but since he hadn't met someone he wanted to spend the rest of his life with, he'd never brought anyone with him. One coworker had tried to set him up, but he'd put an end to that immediately as well.

"You put my yoga instructor to shame."

Sambit looked up from a monkey pose to see Lyrica standing in the corridor. "I've been doing yoga since I could walk," he explained. "My mother started every day with fifteen minutes of yoga and ended it with an hour. It's a habit I never saw a reason to break."

"No reason why you should," Lyrica said. "If we end up here for very long, I may join you. I go to classes twice a week."

"You're welcome to join me anytime," Sambit said. "I'm hoping Derek will join me as well."

"Good luck on that one," Lyrica said with a shake of her head. "I've been around good ol' boys like him my whole life. They'll do many things, but yoga isn't one of them. Not even when they're gay."

"What does being gay have to do with it?" Sambit asked.

"Nothing," Lyrica said, "but these Texas boys, they don't see yoga as a 'real' sport so it's something for the girls to do, not something any self-respecting man would be caught doing."

Sambit's opinion of Derek went up a little more. "Derek did a few asanas with me, although perhaps you shouldn't mention it. I thought it might help his stress level. I still think it will if he'll do it regularly."

"I'm impressed," Lyrica said. "Either you're very persuasive or he likes you."

"Your guess is as good as mine," Sambit said quickly, not wanting to encourage speculation about Derek's motivations for the little bit of yoga he'd done earlier. The protectiveness surprised him after everything Derek had done to try and alienate Sambit when they first met. Sambit chalked it up to the moments of vulnerability when Derek let down his guard and talked to Fido. "We should probably try to get some sleep. I imagine Tucker will be in here in a couple of hours demanding we fix whatever problems the other team finds since they don't have Derek's robot."

"I only hope he doesn't decide to be a hero and make matters worse," Lyrica said. "Maybe I should have a word with Thomas. He's the next senior employee present. I don't know if he'd stand up to Tucker on his own, but maybe he will on my authority if I tell him not to attempt any repairs he can't do through the servers."

"I'm going to set up my cot. Shall I set one up for you as well?"

"Sure," Lyrica said, "preferably where I have a good view of Derek's boys. They'll make for pleasant dreams in the middle of this nightmare."

"As long as you dream about his pinups and not about him," Sambit said with a laugh. "No reason to set yourself up for heartbreak."

"And what will *you* be dreaming about?" Lyrica asked.

"I don't dream." Sambit wasn't about to go down that line of questioning.

"Everyone dreams."

Sambit shrugged. "Then I don't remember them. I'll get your cot ready." He walked back in the break room before she could say anything else.

"I thought I'd set cots for Lyrica and me up over here," he said to Derek. "That way we're a little bit out of the way if the others need to come in during their shift, and vice versa when it's our shift."

"Knock yourself out," Derek said. "Anything that keeps that prick Jeremiah as far away from me as possible."

"He never would have known if you were a little more discreet," Sambit said. "You wouldn't have to deal with his attitude if he didn't know."

"So he has the right to rub his piety in my face and I'm supposed to just live with it?" Derek snapped. "Fuck that. At least this way he hates me for a reason and knows why I hate him."

"His hatred is his own problem," Sambit said. "You don't have to fan it."

"So you'd choose calm over honesty?" Derek demanded.

"It's always worked for me."

"Yeah, well, it didn't work for me. I tried leaving people alone and minding my own business. They came at me until I snapped. I guess that's the difference between being gay and just being different."

"You're making an awfully big assumption there," Sambit said, bracing for the explosion to come. Derek wouldn't care that he was gay, but Derek would undoubtedly have a few things to say about his decision not to flaunt that fact.

It took a minute for that to sink in past Derek's temper, but Sambit could tell the moment it did because Derek's expression hardened. "If you're yanking my chain, stop it right the fuck now. If you're telling me you're gay too, get the hell out of my sight."

"Why?" Sambit demanded, not sure why he wasn't willing to simply give Derek what he wanted. "Why can't I choose to be discreet rather than combative about something that's no one's business but mine and my lover's?"

"Because it's a cowardly betrayal of those of us who are out there fighting for our rights," Derek spat. "You reap the benefits without taking any of the risks."

"I never asked anyone to take any risks for me," Sambit said. "I didn't ask for more rights or different treatment or anything other than what I have as a holder of a green card. If I eventually become a citizen, perhaps I will feel differently, but for now, I am more than content as I am."

"You don't want to get married someday?" Derek asked. "Or have the right to let your partner make decisions for you if you're incapacitated? Or be able to provide health insurance for your partner? Or all the other rights straight couples get the moment they decide to spend their lives together?"

"I have no partner, as you put it," Sambit said, "and even if I did, my family would never allow him to make decisions for me. They might consult my wife if I had one, but the decisions would not be hers alone. Families don't work that way in India."

"You don't live in India."

"Not at the moment," Sambit agreed, "but I don't know what the future holds. India has many nuclear power plants. I may tire of teaching and decide to return there to work. If I do, this entire conversation will be moot. Even if you get your wish and Texas allows gay marriage, it would not be recognized in India. My partner would have even fewer rights there than he would have here."

"And you're just willing to accept that," Derek said. "I don't get people like you. How can you just bend over and let the system fuck you?"

Sambit sighed. "Must you curse constantly? It doesn't make your point any more forcefully. Indeed, it undermines your argument, because all I hear is the vulgarity rather than any logic that might be embedded in what you're saying."

"That's your problem, not mine."

"It's not my problem at all," Sambit retorted. "I can simply choose to ignore you. If you wish to persuade me, however, you must retain my attention and convince me of your point of view. You have not done that if you lose my attention because of your choice of language."

"So why don't you just walk away?"

Why don't I? Sambit had no answer to the question, yet he couldn't make himself turn around and walk out, and not just because he had nowhere else to go.

"Because you would take that as a victory as well," Sambit said finally. "You would congratulate yourself on having driven me off, and I refuse to let you win that way."

"Do you really want to turn this into a pissing match?"

"No." Sambit already knew he'd lose that battle. "I prefer to turn this into a working relationship that keeps the reactor from melting down and doesn't turn the control room into a war zone. However, I need a little help to make that happen. I'm happy to meet you halfway, but I can't do it alone."

"Maybe we both need a little more of that yoga."

Sambit took that as the olive branch it was, nodding and bending to pet Fido. "You could have picked a less generic name."

"I could have left him in the house where I found him."

"No, you couldn't have." Sambit didn't know a lot of things about Derek Marshall, but he knew that much. No matter what else, Derek wouldn't leave someone in danger if he could help. "You don't have that much cruelty in you. You might leave me, but you wouldn't leave a dog."

"I wouldn't leave you." The scowl on Derek's face amused Sambit. The other man obviously hadn't intended to say that out loud.

"Tucker, perhaps?"

"Tucker for sure, and Jeremiah," Derek said, crossing his arms defensively. "You annoy me, but you don't piss me off."

"I'm flattered," Sambit said with a laugh. Deciding not to push his luck, he grabbed two of the folded-up cots, setting them up near Derek's. He left the Army-issue blankets on one of them, but he took his time spreading them out neatly on the other. Anything to give himself a little more time before he had to face Derek again. When he couldn't mess with the blankets anymore, he found the small suitcase he'd packed and moved it under the cot, pulling his toothbrush out of the front pocket and using the sink in the break room to brush his teeth. He glanced at Derek as he put his toothbrush away. Derek hadn't moved from his seat on the cot.

"If I try not to curse as much, will you teach me more of that yoga like we did earlier?"

"In the morning," Sambit said. "We're both tired tonight. Yoga is not an exercise to do when your mind is fatigued. If you cannot concentrate on doing it correctly, you could make a mistake and hurt yourself. We should take Fido out one more time so he will sleep through the night."

"We?" Derek asked.

"I will take him myself if you would prefer," Sambit said. "You've already been outside once today with no radiation gear. You shouldn't do that too often."

"He's my dog, not yours."

"So he is, but I can help, can't I?"

"But why would you?" Derek asked.

"Because it's the right thing to do," Sambit said. "Just like rescuing him in the first place."

"You are a strange, strange man, Sambit Patel."

Sambit grinned. "But you like me anyway."

"Maybe I do at that."

SAMBIT awoke at his usual time the next morning, rising and stretching lightly to get his circulation moving. He could hear Derek's light snores in the darkness and Lyrica's softer breathing as well as Fido's occasional snuffle. He debated leaving Derek to sleep a little longer rather than waking him, but Derek had asked, and Sambit didn't want to make matters worse between them. He padded softly to Derek's side, bending to pat Fido's head so the dog wouldn't growl or bark and wake everyone else up too. Then he nudged Derek gently until the snores stopped and Derek rolled over.

"Wha' time is't?"

"Six a.m.," Sambit replied. "You said you wanted to do yoga with me this morning. This is what time I get up."

"Don't tell me you're a fucking morning person."

"I thought you were going to try not to curse so much," Sambit teased, ignoring the question inherent in Derek's words.

"Not if you wake me up at six in the morning," Derek grumbled. "I suppose that means you don't have coffee for me either."

"No coffee or tea until after yoga," Sambit said. "You don't want to be halfway through pigeon and have to go to the bathroom."

"Pigeon?" Derek asked, sitting up slowly and scrubbing at his face with his hands. "I'm in way over my head, aren't I?"

"I'll go easy on you the first time," Sambit said, "but don't expect me to cut you any slack tomorrow."

Derek groaned and stood up. "All right. Torture me."

Derek's sleepy face as he spoke sent wildly inappropriate thoughts through Sambit's mind. He was glad he had slept in his pants rather than in just his boxers as he would usually do. He'd be leaving them on to stretch, too, if his body was going to react this way. He didn't need to give Derek ideas.

"Let's go out in the hallway," he said. "That way we won't wake Lyrica up."

To Sambit's surprise, Derek remembered the Surya Namaskar from the day before, moving through the twelve postures of the sun salutation with much greater ease than he had the first time. Sambit wasn't sure if that was his natural athleticism coming out or if he was simply more relaxed this morning, but either way, Derek's movements were much closer to the thing of reverent beauty they were intended to be.

When they had finished four sets, Sambit smiled. "How do you feel?"

Derek paused a moment, taking stock of his body. "Pretty good, actually. I always stretch before and after I run, not that I'll be running here anytime soon. This is a little more intense than what I do, but it's the same muscles for the most part, and after several days of being cooped up inside, it feels good to use them."

"That's one of the things I like about yoga. All you need is enough space."

"And someone who knows what they're doing," Derek said. "I wouldn't know where to begin without you here to tell me what to do."

"Give it a few days," Sambit said, "and you'll know enough to do a full, if basic, workout without me. Ready for something a little more challenging?"

"I'm always up for a challenge."

Sambit had already learned how true that was, even after less than twenty-four hours. Grinning with mischief, he slid down into Hanumanasana, his legs in a complete split, his arms overhead as he arched his back. When he had his balance, he looked up at Derek. "Well, what are you waiting for?"

"You're going to have to offer me a hell of a lot more than you have if you want me to spread my legs like that," Derek retorted.

Sambit shook his head. He should have known Derek would turn it into something suggestive. Well, two could play that game. "And what, exactly, are your requirements for spreading your legs?" He curled out of the monkey pose and rolled back into plow pose, his feet touching the ground above his head.

"If you keep sticking your ass in the air like that, Sam, I'm going to get ideas."

"Talk, talk, talk," Sambit teased. "I thought you wanted to do yoga."

"The human body is not meant to bend like that."

"Sure it is," Sambit said, rolling out of the pose and assuming the lotus position. "You just have to teach it how. We'll start with something a little more basic and work up to more advanced poses later."

Derek looked skeptical. Amused, but skeptical.

"Sit down," Sambit urged. "We'll do some forward bends and backbends. Go as far as you can into the pose and then stop. You don't have to do everything I can do the first time you try. I started doing yoga as a child with my mother over thirty years ago. I could barely walk, but I could sit in a lotus pose by the time I was a year old."

"Maybe that's why you couldn't walk," Derek grumbled as he tried to imitate Sambit's crossed legs.

"Don't go that far yet," Sambit said when he saw the grimace on Derek's face. He reached over and pulled Derek's hand off the foot he was trying to raise onto his opposite knee. "For now, do a half lotus, just one foot on top of your thigh with the other underneath. We'll switch in a moment, and that will stretch both hips and ankles."

Derek's skepticism didn't fade, but he moved as Sambit directed.

"I like this biddable side of you," Sambit joked. "You should follow directions this well in other contexts too."

"If I did that, we'd be stuck following Tucker's orders instead of doing what really needs to be done," Derek replied.

"True," Sambit had to agree. "But you could maybe try following Lyrica's directions today?"

"Unless you tell me to do something different," Derek said.

That was enough to stun Sambit into silence. He wrestled with the potential implications of that one sentence for the rest of their yoga workout and all the way through breakfast. When they reported to the control room to take over from the other team, he was no closer to having an answer than when Derek had first said it.

chapter
SIX

BY THE time they took a quick break for lunch, Derek's good mood from the morning had worn off. Tucker had been even more officious and offensive than the day before, insisting they follow protocol to the letter even when Lyrica and Sambit both argued for quicker action. Derek would have bucked Tucker's authority on his own, but he didn't know what to do without either Lyrica or Sambit directing him, and Tucker had kept them from doing that.

"What are we going to do about that shmuck?" Derek asked as they ate their canned soup in the hallway outside the break room where the other team was sleeping. "We aren't getting anything done today because he won't let us, and I know the situation didn't drastically improve overnight."

"I can try going over his head," Lyrica said, "but that could backfire on us. At the moment we're working around him when we can because no one's told us not to. If I go to my boss or his boss and they say we have to follow his directions exactly, I won't have any choice but to listen."

"I don't have to," Derek said.

"No, but you still need us to tell you what to do."

"Sambit?" Derek asked. "What do you think?"

"I think we're gambling with our lives here already," Sambit said slowly. "We haven't had enough exposure yet, I don't think, to worry about acute radiation sickness, but it's building up in our systems, doing a little damage here and a little damage there. The sooner we can get things under control and get ourselves far away from here, the better."

"So what do you suggest?" Lyrica asked.

"The core temperatures have stayed within expected range overnight," Sambit said, "so the boron injections we did yesterday are working. I'm not saying the danger is past because it won't be until we have the entire system cooled down, but it's on the right track. The greater concern, from where I'm sitting, is the breach in the secondary containment system and the Standby Gas Treatment system. We know there was at least some radiation leakage because of the numbers we saw yesterday, and without the SGT online, that radiation is getting out into the environment."

"So how do we fix it?" Derek asked.

"That's where it gets complicated," Lyrica said. "We know there was a leak, and we know it's getting out into the environment through the breach in the secondary containment system, but we don't know where it's coming from in the first place. The secondary containment system is a backup. It shouldn't have to contain that level of radiation except in case of an emergency."

"Which this is."

"Which this is," Lyrica agreed with a nod in Derek's direction. "We need to find where the radiation is coming from in the first place. That's where we have to concentrate our efforts."

"So we need to get Tucker to let us go exploring," Derek replied, "either in person or with Number Five. My guess is he's not going to approve us going in person."

"After yesterday?" Lyrica said with a bitter laugh. "He's got the hazmat suits under lock and key. We won't get anywhere near them without his approval, and we won't get anywhere near the source and survive without them, based on the Geiger counter readings yesterday."

"Then we have to get Number Five where we can't go," Derek said. "How do we get around Tucker long enough to do what we need to do without him barging in and stopping us?"

"You could try pissing him off to the point that he storms off and calls your boss," Lyrica said.

"I could, but if he drags me with him to talk to Kenneth, I won't be there to operate the robot."

"And don't expect me to operate it in his place," Sambit added. "I'd never get where we were going."

"We need a diversion," Derek said. "I don't suppose we can just throw Tucker in a closet and lock him in for a couple of hours."

"I'd prefer a diversion that didn't cost me my job," Lyrica said with a shake of her head. "I'll just have to take one for the team. I can get Tucker into a debate about regulations, insist he show me the protocols for everything. You don't need the main computers to work with Number Five. You can do that from anywhere, right?"

Derek nodded.

"So you two go somewhere else and see what you can find," Lyrica directed. "Take Number Five out the way we went and in through the hole in the secondary containment system. Hopefully you can track down the leak."

"Then we have to convince Tucker to let us fix it."

"If we can identify the source of the leak, he has to let us fix it," Lyrica said. "Right now he's trying to deny that there is a leak because he wasn't out there with us. He thinks it'll make him look bad to have a leak on a project he's overseeing."

"Maybe so, but wouldn't it look better to find and contain a leak than have it cause environmental problems?" Derek asked.

"You'd think," Lyrica said, "but hiding his head in the sand seems to be more his style. Of course I'm sure he'll be happy to take all the credit if we do manage to find and fix the leak."

"I don't need credit," Derek said. "I need not to die here."

Lyrica laughed, the sound rueful. "That's one way of putting it. Okay, let's go see if I can keep Tucker occupied for a while. Where are you two going to set up?"

"In the break room," Derek said. "He tries to avoid going in there out of respect for the off-shift people. Sam and I shouldn't need to talk much, so we won't disturb them either."

"And if they wake up and see you?" Lyrica asked. "Melanie and Thomas might not care, but you've made enough of an enemy of Jeremiah that he'd run and tell Tucker just to spite you."

"Where else is there?" Derek asked.

Lyrica grinned. "Well, there's the janitor's closet. It's not glamorous, but I can guarantee Tucker won't look for you there."

"And neither will anyone else," Derek said, returning her grin. "Well, Sam, shall we go back in the closet for a couple of hours?"

To Derek's surprise, Sambit grinned too. "I thought you hated the closet."

It was those little bits of humor that always caught Derek off guard. He had this image of Sambit, lingering from their first meeting, of a starchy, buttoned-up, prim man, and while that was true in some respects, Derek was discovering how untrue it was in others. Sambit might be prim, but he wasn't repressed, and underneath that proper exterior lay a wicked sense of humor. "Only if I'm forced into it," Derek replied. "I've found closets quite interesting when I choose my company."

"Oh, really?" Sambit said, finishing his tea and standing up. "I don't remember you choosing my company."

"I got up at six a.m. to do yoga with you," Derek reminded him, tossing his bowl in the trash. With no running water because of the flooding, they couldn't wash dishes and had to use disposable ones instead. "If that isn't choosing your company, I don't know what is."

"Why, Mr. Marshall, I didn't realize what an honor that was," Sambit simpered, batting his eyelashes at Derek.

Lyrica burst out laughing, breaking the sudden tension that invested Derek's frame at Sambit's flirting, however jokingly. "You two are something else. The closet is at the end of the hallway on the left. Get your computer and get started while I go distract Tucker."

"I'll get the computer," Sambit offered. "You get Number Five outside and join me."

"Sounds good," Derek said, still a little off kilter from the unexpected banter. He took a few deep breaths as he walked into the break room and unplugged Number Five from where it was charging, trying to dismiss his sudden susceptibility to Sambit's teasing. The other man wasn't at all Derek's type, except that appearances, in this case, were deceiving. Sambit didn't look like Derek's type, but he was acting more and more like the kind of man Derek could be very attracted to. Of course there was the issue of Sambit being essentially in the closet, and the fact that Derek had no idea if Sambit found him attractive in return. Oh, and the fact that they could all die of radiation sickness if the core had a meltdown or if the radiation leak got worse.

He couldn't think about that or he'd go crazy or go looking for a bottle of booze. They'd been careful, and his Geiger counter had only beeped when he was wearing the hazmat suit, so he hoped they were safe. The dosimeter on his belt that measured his personal exposure to radiation over time hadn't sounded any kind of alert. Maybe he'd look into radiation sickness a little later, though. Just so he knew what signs to watch for.

He carried Number Five to the door and set the robot down outside, glancing at his Geiger counter out of habit, but the readings, while higher than inside, were not at dangerous levels. He took a moment more to make sure Number Five was receiving the signals from his remote, then went in search of the janitor's closet and Sambit.

"So what are we looking for?" Derek asked as he maneuvered in the small space to find a spot where he could see the computer screen and still sit comfortably.

"Anything that isn't as it should be," Sambit said.

"That's so helpful," Derek joked, "since I don't know what anything is supposed to look like. Lyrica said to start where the containment system was damaged, right?"

"Right," Sambit said. "That's where we have the highest radiation levels so far. If we can trace that back to the source, we should be able to find the leak."

"Okay, let's do it."

Derek guided Number Five across the open space, noticing that the puddles weren't quite as numerous or as deep as they'd been the day before. "It looks like the flooding is going down."

"As long as we don't get hit again with runoff from inland," Sambit agreed. "The Colorado River isn't very far away."

"One disaster at a time, please," Derek said, navigating around the rubble that had killed the second shift manager. "Two at a time might be more than I could handle."

"I don't believe that for a moment," Sambit said. Derek gave him a sharp look but let it go for the moment. This wasn't the time to discuss the new awareness that had plagued Derek since their yoga session that morning.

"Okay, here's where the Geiger counter went ballistic yesterday," Derek said. "Number Five's readings aren't quite as high as the Geiger counter said, but they're still higher than they were when I first put it outside."

Sambit accepted the change of subject without comment, focusing back on the computer screen and what he could see through the robot's cameras. "Radiation can come from two places: the reactor itself and the spent fuel rods. I haven't even asked Lyrica if anyone checked on the spent rods, other than when we put her colleague in there to get him out of the elements, but I don't think that's the source of our problem. I think we've got a valve that's leaking or something like that."

"A crack in the core?"

"No, if we had that, the pressure inside would be out of balance. Once we put the boron solution in, it's stayed within a predictable range, so the core is intact."

"I thought the computer systems were supposed to monitor the valves and stuff for leaks." Derek guided Number Five deeper into the secondary containment system. The Geiger counter readings stayed fairly stable, so while he wasn't sure they were moving closer to the source, he figured they weren't moving farther from it.

"They are," Sambit said, "but we've already gotten inconsistent readings from the system in other areas. We can't afford to rely on those readings until we've verified them."

"So what are we looking for?" Derek asked again.

"At the moment, a spike in the radiation levels," Sambit said. "Something to give us a clue where to look more closely."

"So I'll just keep letting Number Five wander."

Sambit nodded, and Derek let silence fall between them.

"You realize that after that conversation, Lyrica probably knows you're gay too," he said eventually.

"I told you. I don't deny that I'm gay. I simply don't choose to broadcast it to every person I meet regardless of their need to know or the impact their knowing might have on me," Sambit replied. "I'm not pretending to be someone I'm not. I'm choosing who I show certain sides of myself to, the same as I choose who I show my sense of humor to, or who I tell about my childhood in India. If Lyrica knows now, that's fine. If she doesn't, that's also fine. She can draw what conclusions she chooses to. If they are incorrect ones and it interferes with our working relationship, I will correct them, but until then, it doesn't matter."

"How can it not matter how people see you?" Derek asked, puzzled rather than angry now that the initial, ingrained reaction to Sambit's revelation had worn off.

"Because how they see me doesn't affect who I am," Sambit explained. "I don't define myself by how others see me. I know the truth about myself, and nothing else matters. If someone makes a false assumption and it affects how we interact—if a woman flirts with me and won't take no for an answer, for example—I might correct that assumption, but most of the time, those interactions are too fleeting or inconsequential to make it worth the effort. Whether I say I'm not interested or I'm gay, the result is the same, so why make it into a bigger issue than it is?"

"Because if she knows you're gay, she might introduce you to her cute brother," Derek said, but Sambit didn't smile at Derek's attempt at a joke. "Okay, sorry, that was lame."

"You didn't answer my question."

Derek sighed and tried to formulate an explanation for his experiences and convictions. "I tried ignoring how others saw me," he said slowly. "I tried to ignore the comments and taunts and assumptions, the jocks who figured that because I was gay, I'd be willing to blow them when they couldn't get a girl to do it. I was a cocksucker so why not suck theirs? I tried to ignore the jeers when I walked down the school halls and they crucified me for being smart at the same time they crucified me for being gay. I tried letting that roll off my back, and nothing changed. So I went away to college where at least being smart didn't make me different. Being gay still did, and hiding it didn't work because people found out, and then they accused me of lying because I hadn't told them. I got tired of it. If I put it all out there up front, no one can accuse me of lying. No one can accuse me of being something I'm not."

"I can see that helping with the people who accused you of lying, but how does it change the way the jocks treated you in high school?" Sambit asked. "Their actions came from their assumptions about what it means to be gay, not from anything you said or did or didn't say or do."

"I'm a little stronger now than I was then. They can't force me onto my knees anymore."

EVERYTHING made so much more sense now.

That was Sambit's first thought when the import of Derek's words sank in. His second thought was outrage at the thought of anyone being subjected to that kind of abuse. "Did you report them?"

"Of course I did," Derek said. "You know what the coach told me? They didn't mean anything by it. It was just a bit of harmless roughhousing. Boys will be boys, after all."

"What about the principal? Or the police?" Sambit asked.

"It was my word against theirs," Derek said bitterly. "There was no physical evidence other than a bruise on my knee that could have come from anywhere, and those were the boys who were going to win us a state championship in football this year. Nothing could be allowed to jeopardize that."

"For what it's worth, and I realize that's probably nothing, I believe you," Sambit said. He wanted to reach over and comfort Derek, but the hurt was hardly new and the other man was already so prickly that Sambit didn't want to make it worse.

"It's old news," Derek said.

Sambit might have believed that if Derek hadn't retreated behind his defensive mask again. The sudden beeping of the robot's Geiger counter interrupted them before Sambit could figure out what to say next.

"What the hell?" Derek demanded.

"I don't know," Sambit said. "Give me a minute."

"At those levels of radiation, a minute is all you're going to get before the circuits are fried. I don't have a backup robot."

"Okay, get him out of there," Sambit said. "I'll study the video he took and hope I can see something from that."

He waited while Derek directed the robot back out of the secondary containment system. "With that kind of exposure, it'll have to stay outside until we can get a hazmat suit to take off its shell," Sambit said. "We can't work on it without one."

"Which means dealing with Tucker," Derek said with a groan. "I hope to Christ we got something useful in the videos because I don't want to have to fight with that asshole for nothing."

"We have the Geiger counter readings if nothing else," Sambit said. "They're proof that we have a problem. Let me look at the footage and see if I can spot what's causing it."

Derek hit play on the recordings Number Five had made, scooting back so Sambit could peer more closely at the screen, watching the corresponding Geiger counter numbers as he studied the frames. "I don't see anything out of place other than the outer wall," Sambit said finally. "The turbine, the condenser, the generator all look exactly like I would expect them to look under the circumstances."

"Could they have gotten irradiated somehow?" Derek asked.

"Obviously they did," Sambit said. "The question is how. There shouldn't be any transfer between the reactor and the turbines. The whole point of a pressurized water reactor is to keep all radioactive material confined within the reactor building."

"So what brings the heat out, then?" Derek asked. "I mean, it's steam from the heat of the nuclear reaction that turns the turbines, right?"

"Yes, that's right," Sambit said. "There's a transference system within the reactor building where the heated coolant from the core runs through pipes surrounded by water. That water produces the steam that comes out to the turbines."

"So what would happen if some of those pipes were damaged?" Derek asked. "Could the water and the coolant get mixed together so that some of the radioactive material could end up in the turbine area?"

"If so, the plant is fucked," Sambit said. "There's no way to get in there for repairs. This unit will have to be decommissioned like the one that melted down on Three Mile Island."

"I thought you didn't curse," Derek teased.

"You must be rubbing off on me," Sambit replied, summoning a smile.

"Not until we've had a chance to shower, thank you," Derek joked. "Neither one of us smells particularly pleasant at the moment, I imagine."

Sambit boggled at the speed Derek changed moods. From vulnerable to defensive to flirtatious in the span of minutes. He couldn't decide if that made the other man infuriating or fascinating. Or both.

"And here I thought getting sweaty and dirty was the point," Sambit replied, not sure where the boldness came from but unwilling to let the moment pass.

"You're supposed to end up sweaty and sticky," Derek agreed, "but I can only deal with so many days of body odor when I start, and I passed that point two days ago."

Sambit laughed and shook his head. "You win. Let's get Number Five unwrapped and see if we can figure out any other explanation for the radioactivity around the turbine before we give Tucker the bad news."

"I can't help you figure out the explanation," Derek said. "I'll deal with Number Five because I want to run some diagnostics anyway. You and Lyrica can come find me when you have something I can actually help with."

"You just don't want to deal with Tucker."

"There is that," Derek agreed, "but I really should check the circuits in Number Five. They aren't built to withstand that kind of radiation for long."

"Put a hazmat suit on, at least a lower grade one since Tucker hasn't bothered locking those up, before you take the covering off Number Five," Sambit said. "If that kind of radiation could damage Number Five, just think about what it could do to you."

Derek looked down at his dosimeter. "I'm thinking."

chapter
SEVEN

DEREK spent two hours running diagnostics on Number Five, switching out circuits, cleaning and oiling gears, and generally doing everything he could to avoid having to go find Lyrica and Sambit while they argued with Tucker. He couldn't follow the conversation, but he heard raised voices now and then, enough to let him know they were indeed arguing.

When he finished with Number Five, he opened a browser and searched for information on radiation sickness. Not that he thought they were in any immediate danger, since their dosimeters measured how much radiation exposure they'd had since they arrived and they hadn't sounded any alarms, but he wanted to know what to watch for just in case. He read one article and shut the browser, sick to his stomach at everything he'd seen. Nausea, vomiting, headaches, fever, dizziness, cognitive impairment.

Death.

He'd known that before he came. He remembered reading about Hiroshima in his history classes and the effects, both immediate and lingering, of the bombs dropped there and in Nagasaki. He just hadn't thought about it in connection with himself. Not really.

He ought to call his mother, just in case. He couldn't tell her where he was or what he was doing, but he could tell her he loved her so that if he didn't make it, they'd be the last words he said to her. "Come here, Fido," he called, needing the reassurance of the dog's company.

Fido stood up from where he'd been sleeping just beyond Derek's reach and padded closer, laying his head on Derek's lap. Derek rested his forehead against Fido's shoulder and stroked the solid body. He couldn't die. He had to take care of Fido, radiation sickness be damned. He'd simply have to dodge that bullet one way or another.

"That's a very comforting sight."

Derek looked up from Fido's side to see Sambit at the entrance to the room where he was working. His fingers pinched the bridge of his nose, and the corners of his mouth were tight. "What did Tucker say?"

"He ranted for a while about exceeding our authority by taking Number Five out without his permission," Sambit began.

"Fuck that," Derek said. "Number Five answers to me, and I don't answer to him."

"He thinks you do," Sambit said with a sigh. "When he was done with that tirade, he started in on the readings and the conclusions we drew based on them. He challenged the accuracy of them, although Lyrica shot that down pretty quickly by citing the readings on our Geiger counters when we went outside yesterday. Then he blew off the suggestion that the system was compromised. He has one goal, as far as I can tell. To get the plant running again."

"That would be fine if it weren't dangerous," Derek said. "Can't he focus on getting the other two running again and let this one close?"

"You'd think so," Sambit said, rubbing his temples.

"Is your head bothering you?" Derek asked sharply, the descriptions he'd read too fresh in his brain to ignore the signs.

"It's just stress from dealing with Tucker."

"Maybe it is, but headaches are also a sign of radiation sickness," Derek said, his stomach churning at the thought of Sambit coming down with the awful symptoms he'd read about.

"It is, but I'm not nauseated, and that precedes the headaches," Sambit said.

"Are you sure?" Derek said. "I mean, I know it usually does, but isn't it possible that you skipped a step?"

"I suppose it's possible," Sambit said, "but my dosimeter readings aren't anywhere near the levels they would need to be for the radiation to make me sick."

"Yes, but everyone is different. It makes sense that people would react differently. Do we need to call a doctor?"

"Derek, I'm fine," Sambit said. "I'll take an Advil and lie down in a quiet, dark room for an hour or two, and I'll be all better."

Derek hesitated for a moment, but the need to help outweighed the fear of being refused. "I could rub your shoulders for you if you think it would help. If it's really tension and not radiation, it might help you relax."

"If you don't mind," Sambit said. "Usually I would try meditation or some stretches, but I usually get to that point before my headache gets this bad. I'm not sure mind over matter will be very successful when my mind hurts too much to concentrate."

"Take off your shirt," Derek directed, "the outer one at least. You can leave your undershirt if you'd be more comfortable."

Sambit shook his head, unbuttoning the oxford shirt he wore and tossing it aside before stripping off his undershirt. Derek had seen him without the outer shirt yesterday, and he'd felt his own muscles strain as they practiced yoga that morning, barely able to hold some of the strength poses that Sambit did with ease, so he knew Sambit had to have some muscle, but that didn't prepare him for the sheer beauty of the bare torso. His chest, not darkened by the sun, was closer to the color of teak than mahogany, with a patch of dark hair in a triangle across it, narrowing to a thin band that arrowed down into the waistband of his trousers. He could have posed for any of Derek's magazines in a heartbeat.

"Lie down," Derek suggested. "You'll be more comfortable, and if you fall asleep, you can stay there instead of having to move later."

"Let me take some Advil and then I will," Sambit said. Derek watched as Sambit dug in his bag and fished out the analgesic. He swallowed it dry and stretched out on the cot, twisting one way and then the other as he tried to get settled. Derek told himself to stop being ridiculous as his mouth watered at the sight. Sambit may have been lying down, but he wasn't lying down *for* Derek, not in that sense. He was getting ready for a backrub intended to ease a tension headache. Nothing more.

So why did it feel like so much more?

Derek closed one hand around the back of Sambit's neck, kneading the tight muscles with firm pressure. Sambit's skin was warm beneath the pads of Derek's fingers, the fine hairs on the nape of his neck creating an erotic friction against Derek's skin despite his determination to keep this friendly, nothing more. He took a deep breath, smelling the spicy hint of days-old cologne beneath the sweat on both their bodies, and it added to the growing sense of intimacy. Ordering himself to concentrate on the matter at hand and not on all the lascivious things he'd do if the situation—and the man—were different, he moved his hand down to Sambit's shoulder, his other hand joining the first to work at releasing the tension in the tight muscles. Sambit might be gay after all, and he might even be willing to give Derek a chance in this arena, but a relationship couldn't work between them, and Sambit wasn't the type for a fling. Derek might be more adrift than he'd felt in years where another man was concerned, but he didn't think he'd lost all judgment about his potential partners.

"You feel awfully warm," Derek said as he continued the massage. "Are you sure you aren't feverish?"

"There are other reasons besides a fever to have heated skin," Sambit said softly, his eyes closed and his face composed so that Derek didn't know how to interpret that. He knew how he'd *like* to interpret it, but Sambit couldn't be flirting with him in earnest. Could he? "My normal body temperature is about a degree above everyone else's. No one's ever been able to figure out why, but I always feel like I have a low-grade fever when that's just the way I am."

That shot down the flirting idea.

"Okay, just checking," Derek said in a strangled voice. "Fever is another sign of radiation sickness."

"Derek, I teach future nuclear engineers," Sambit said. "We drum the symptoms of radiation sickness—and the need to pay attention to those symptoms—into them from the very beginning, and we don't let up until they leave us four to six years later. I promise I'm paying attention, but I know my own body, and this is a tension headache, probably coupled with sinus pain from the changing weather and the humidity. I feel feverish because it's hot and because my skin is always warm to the touch, even when it's cold outside. I'm not nauseated, and

I haven't had anywhere near a dangerous dose of radiation. Now stop fretting and either finish the massage or let me go to sleep."

"I ought to leave you to deal with the headache by yourself," Derek huffed, but he didn't move away, his hands continuing the massage farther down Sambit's back. He pressed a little harder along Sambit's spine, listening to the joints pop at the compression.

Sambit gasped softly and then sighed. "Oh, that feels good. I've had a cramp there all day that I couldn't get rid of."

"Glad I could help," Derek said. "Anywhere else in particular, or should I just keep going?"

"Just keep going," Sambit said. "It feels really good."

"I dated a masseur at one point," Derek explained. "He gave me some tips after the first disaster of a backrub I gave him. I'm not a professional, but I can generally make my victim feel pretty relaxed."

"Your victim?" Sambit asked, amused.

"Well, what else should I call you?" Derek replied. "I'm not a pro, so you aren't a client or a patient. You aren't my lover, even if that's who I usually use my skills on. I couldn't think of anything else."

"I see your point," Sambit said after a moment's silence. "Victim it is."

Derek kneaded his way back up Sambit's spine to his shoulders again, focusing a little more on Sambit's trapezius muscles and neck. "There," he said finally. "All better?"

Sambit rolled onto his back, his eyes even darker than usual—not that Derek had noticed or anything—and stared up at Derek. "Much better, thank you."

Derek focused diligently on Sambit's face rather than letting his eyes wander lower over the rest of Sambit's body, so it caught him off guard when Sambit slid his hand around Derek's and held on tight.

"What?" Derek asked, not sure why Sambit had such a grip on him.

Sambit didn't reply, his eyes searching Derek's face as if looking for something, but Derek had no idea what, and the intensity of Sambit's gaze made him nervous. "Did I break out in zits or something?"

Sambit hushed him softly, his grip remaining firm. The urge to pull away and run grew nearly irresistible for Derek, but Sambit's hand steadied him, and so he sat there, trapped by the simple touch and powerful gaze.

"I wish we'd met in different circumstances," Sambit said finally.

"Why's that?" Derek asked.

"Because if we had, you never would have given me the time of day."

"What's that supposed to mean?" Derek asked.

"It means you make me want impossible things," Sambit said, sitting up with a sigh. "If we'd met elsewhere, professionally or socially, you would have dismissed me as you did initially, and that would have been the end of it for both of us."

"What do I make you want?" Derek asked, his heart in his throat.

"It doesn't matter," Sambit said. "I can't have them even if you were willing to offer them to me. Thank you for the massage. Should I wake you up for yoga in the morning?"

"Yes," Derek said, thoughts whirling out of control as he tried to make sense of their conversation. "I guess… I guess I should let you get some sleep. Feel better."

"Thank you again."

Derek walked out of the room feeling more than a little confused, so he did what he always did when people got to be more than he could handle. He worked on robots. He'd already done all the maintenance he needed to do on Number Five, so he scrounged in his spare parts and started assembling additions for the commercially available robot Tucker had told them that morning would be delivered the next day. It wouldn't be Number Five, but Derek figured he could juice it up a little so it would be able to do some of the grunt work. He could save Number Five for the fine stuff and maybe prevent a little wear and tear in the process. He'd built the robot to be used, but this was rougher work than he'd imagined when he was designing the specs.

As he worked, Fido came in and rested his head on Derek's leg. "You need to go outside, boy?" he asked. "Let me finish this arm and then we'll go. We still can't stay outside long. I'm sorry. I know you need a good run, but it's not safe out there. You can do your business, though."

Fido just sat there patiently as Derek finished the work he was doing. Finally satisfied the arm would function as it was supposed to, Derek set it aside. "Let's go, Fido."

Checking only to make sure his dosimeter was on his belt, Derek opened the door and let Fido bound outside. Derek stayed closer to the door, leaning against the wall of the building and staring up at the stars overhead. The remnants of the hurricane had passed, leaving the sky crystal clear, and with the power out for hundreds of miles around, there was no light pollution to block Derek's view of the stars. Even an hour after the sun had set, it was still hot and muggy, but the smell of smoke had faded now that they had the reactor under control. If they could figure out the radiation leak, they might get out of here in a few days.

As much as the thought of everything that could go wrong made Derek want to be as far away from here as possible, he didn't want the days to pass too quickly. His ramblings turned to the cause of that desire: Sambit. Prim, proper, flexible, flirtatious, aggravating, attractive Sambit.

Sambit who hadn't judged him or pitied him when he'd brought up his past. He had no idea what had possessed him to mention that miserable day. He hadn't talked about it in years. He'd told one boyfriend about it in college, when he'd felt like he had to give a reason for not wanting to blow the guy in the shower. On the bed, where he could be on top and control the motion, sure, but not on his knees in the shower with the guy above him, fucking his mouth with no recourse for Derek if it got to be too much. The guy had looked at him like he was damaged goods. They'd tried to stay the course, but within a month, the guy had gone on to greener pastures.

In retrospect, Derek didn't blame him. They were nineteen and mostly fucking around. Dealing with a victim of abuse—Derek still couldn't make himself use the word rape—who still hadn't gotten over his hang-ups wasn't on the other guy's agenda. Derek had been sure not to mention it since. Until this afternoon when he'd blurted it out, almost defensively.

Sambit hadn't run screaming from the room, and he hadn't patted Derek on the head and told him it couldn't have been as bad as all that.

Then there was the conversation at the end of the massage. Derek had no fucking idea what to make of that. Impossible things. Things Sambit couldn't have even if Derek offered them. What the fuck was that supposed to mean, and who was Sambit to make those decisions anyway? If Derek knew one thing in life, it was that he had to seize opportunity with both hands before it slipped by. Maybe nothing would come of it. Maybe nothing *could* come of it, but Sambit didn't get to make that decision by himself.

Derek whistled sharply for Fido. The dog came running right away. Derek patted him on the head as they walked back inside. "Go lie down," he said as they turned back into the break room. Lyrica was still somewhere else, and the night shift was already on duty, so Derek was alone with Sambit. He stormed across the room and shook Sambit awake.

"You don't get to make decisions for us both by yourself." He waited only until he saw awareness flare in Sambit's eyes to bend his head and take Sambit's mouth in a forceful kiss. Sambit tasted like mint toothpaste when Derek pushed his tongue past pliant lips to stake a claim he hadn't been aware of wanting until he made it. Sambit gasped into the kiss, twisting on the bed, but Derek framed Sambit's face between his hands, holding him still as the kiss stretched out, deepening, pulling back, then deepening again as their tongues tangled.

"You taste like coffee," Sambit said when Derek broke the kiss to breathe.

"Is that a problem?"

"I don't know," Sambit said, pulling Derek closer again. "Let's find out."

Derek joined the kiss again, eager to see where it would take them. It would be easy to brush aside the blanket covering Sambit's chest and caress the skin he had admired earlier, but he held back, not willing to rush the moment. Sambit was kissing him back, and that made this moment perfect as it was. Later they could discuss Sambit's reasons for calling things between them impossible. Later they could debate the pros and cons of any kind of relationship. Later they could decide this would be nothing more than a precious memory, if it came to that, but that was for later. Now was for the world to fall away, leaving them the only two people in the room, in the universe, for all the world outside this space mattered to Derek. When they broke apart again, panting softly, Derek struggled against the panicked need to run from the perfection of the moment since his rational mind pointed out that nothing about it was perfect, but the urge to climb into bed next to Sambit and never move trumped the urge to leave. Not that he gave in to that inclination either, since the Army cot was barely wide enough for one man. It would never hold two. "That was…."

"It was," Sambit agreed, his voice breathless enough to be gratifying. "I doubt it was wise, but it certainly was."

"Why wasn't it wise?" Derek asked, his voice surprisingly level. In the past, a comment like that would have sent him for the door, washing his hands of the man and the situation before they could take root in his heart. He'd sworn a long time ago that if anyone did the leaving, it would be him.

"How can you even ask me that question?" Sambit said, sitting up. "We have nothing in common, we only met through an emergency situation. In a few days, we'll go back to our old lives and this will be nothing more than a brief footnote in a history book somewhere. I'm not out, you're flaming. I'm Indian, you're not. We don't share the same background, the same anything."

"Life will never be boring," Derek quipped.

"Life will never be peaceful," Sambit retorted. "We'd kill each other in a matter of weeks."

"But what a way to go."

Sambit sighed. "Will you be serious for one minute?"

"I am being serious," Derek said, "more serious than I've been about anything. Look, I don't know anything about India beyond what I've seen on TV, but it can't be any more reactionary than east Texas when it comes to homosexuality. You have a green card, a job here, a life here. You don't have to go back to India if you don't want to, and if the Indian community shuns you for being gay, the gay community would be glad to adopt you instead. I'm not saying it would be easy, but it seems awfully cowardly to not even take the chance."

chapter
EIGHT

COWARDLY.

It was a pretty damn good description of all of Sambit's life to date as far as Sambit could tell, but he didn't think Derek would want to hear that. "For one thing, you're leaving as soon as you can get the second robot outfitted," Sambit said. "That's one of the things Lyrica and I spent the afternoon arguing with Tucker about. He thinks you're nonessential personnel and that you're in the way, not to mention a few less flattering opinions."

"They're mutual, I'm sure," Derek said. Sambit shook his head. Derek's boss had to be a saint to deal with his refusal to tolerate any kind of bullshit.

"Whether they are or not isn't the point," Sambit said. "You're leaving in a matter of a few days. I'm not. I could be here for weeks or months more. There's really not a way for me to leave and come back with the roads washed out the way they are, and they aren't going to let you come back even if you could figure out how to get here. Not exactly solid ground to start a relationship on."

"We could text, e-mail, call each other, something," Derek said.

"That's a nice plan," Sambit said, "but how long do you think it would last? We have nothing in common, Derek. How many times do I have to say that?"

"A few more, apparently," Derek said. "Look, you're tired. You have a headache. It's late, and it's been a crazy day. I'll let you sleep on it tonight, but don't give up on me just because it won't be easy.

Sometimes the things that are the hardest are worth the most. Or was your PhD easier than mine?"

"Fuck off," Sambit said, too tired to come up with a wittier response. "Go away."

"What language!" Derek teased before leaning over and kissing Sambit once more, a light, quick kiss that was over almost before Sambit realized it had started. It left him aching for more.

"Dream of me."

Like he'd be able to dream of anything else.

"I don't dream," Sambit said for the second time in two days.

"Then think of me until you fall asleep," Derek said. "I'm going to work on the robot. I'll be in later."

Sambit watched him go in silence before slumping back onto his cot. This was so wrong. The most interesting, if infuriating, man he'd met in years actually appeared interested in him, and Sambit couldn't do a thing about it. Oh, he could probably indulge in a fling for the next few days, but that was the extent of it. He knew better than to expect it to last beyond Derek's departure, and he knew better than to expect that of himself. He didn't do flings for that very reason. He got attached way too easily, and then it ended with his heart bruised, if not broken.

He had to put Derek out of his mind as much as possible while the engineer was still here, and when Derek left, Sambit had to forget about him entirely. Even if Derek left with the best intentions, he'd get back to his real life, to his job at NASA, to his friends, to cleaning up after the hurricane, and he'd be too busy to think of Sambit as more than a passing fancy, if that. Far better to nip this in the bud than to deal with the hurt later.

He sighed and pulled the covers over his shoulders, determined to take his own advice and fall asleep.

IN THE other room, Derek resumed working on parts for the second robot, his mind racing. Fido wandered in and lay down next to him after a few minutes. Derek rubbed the dog's side. "So, Fido," he said as he fiddled with a camera attachment he was trying to install on a thin robotic arm, "how do I convince Sam I'm serious? He thinks I'm going home in a few days—and we'll see about that, mind you—and forget about him. I think he's wrong, but words aren't working, so I'm going to have to try something else. Any suggestions?"

Fido nudged Derek's thigh with his muzzle until Derek stroked his head a few times before returning to work. A moment later, he looked back at the dog. "That's brilliant! A touch here, a caress there. Nothing obvious, just affection." He got the camera installed to his satisfaction and looked around at what else he could work on before he got the actual robot. "Now what can I do?"

Not finding anything else he could prep for the robot, he wandered down the hall to the restroom. He needed a shower, but the power plant didn't have any facilities. He'd have to settle for a sponge bath. Pulling his shirt over his head, he squirted some soap onto a paper towel and scrubbed at his chest and underarms. "If I had my toolbox, I could rig something up in here so we could actually take a shower," he told Fido, who had followed him down the hall. He grinned suddenly. "I bet there's a toolbox in the janitor's closet. I wonder where Lyrica is. She can let me in, and I can get what I need tonight. I'll start first thing in the morning, and we'll have a shower by lunchtime. Think Sam would let me blow him after he's cleaned up? I'm not leaving without getting my hands on him at least once. I don't want him to forget me once I'm gone."

He rinsed off as much as he could in the restroom sink, already looking forward to a real shower. He grimaced at the smelly T-shirt when he put it back on, but he didn't figure Lyrica would appreciate him walking around shirtless, and he didn't want to give Tucker any more reason to try to get rid of him before he'd completed a few little projects. He might have to leave eventually, but before he did, he was going to do everything he could to make the rest of Sambit's sojourn here as comfortable as possible.

He found Lyrica in the control room with Jeremiah, Melanie, and Thomas. Jeremiah scowled at him but didn't say anything, so Derek didn't acknowledge the sour look on his face. "Could I steal you away for a few minutes, Lyrica? I have a couple of questions."

"Sure," Lyrica said. "We were just finishing up here anyway."

When they were out in the hallway, Derek said, "Sam told me about Tucker trying to get me out of here, and I figure I can't fight it forever, but while I'm here, I might be able to do a few other things to make life more comfortable for everyone besides just building my robot."

"What did you have in mind?" Lyrica asked.

"I was thinking a shower, first of all," Derek said. "With permission and the right tools, I could rip out one of the sinks and rig a temporary shower in its place. If I can find some tubing, I might even be able to do it without taking out the sink. It wouldn't be anything fancy, but it would at least be running water from above people's heads. If you're going to be here for months like Sam thinks, you'll need something."

"Permission granted," Lyrica said immediately. "What do you need in terms of tools?"

"I figure the maintenance area ought to have what I need," Derek said. "A wrench and some plumber's tape are all I have to have. And a hammer if I have to break into the wall to reroute the pipes on that one sink."

"Let's hope it doesn't come to that," Lyrica said. "I'll give you permission if it does, but it would be easier to explain a modified sink than a hole in the wall."

"Not to mention that it would be easier work to modify the sink than to reroute a bunch of pipes," Derek agreed. "I was also thinking if I could find some plywood and some two-by-fours, I could make partitions so people could have some privacy, at least visual privacy, around their cots. Maybe they'll bring in trailers or something for you to live in eventually, but until they do, not worrying about the person in the next cot watching you sleep might make life a little more comfortable too."

"Not that I'm complaining," Lyrica said, "but what's with the sudden impulse to helpfulness? I'd think you'd want nothing more than to shake the dust off your feet on the way out of here."

Derek felt his cheeks heat, but he shrugged. "I was in the restroom trying to clean up, and it seemed like the thing to do."

"And this wouldn't have anything to do with Sambit staying?"

"Why would it?" Derek asked, his heart pounding.

"I don't know," Lyrica said. "The fact that he's gay, also unattached, and interested in you?"

"How do you know that?"

"I didn't just fall off the turnip truck, Marshall. I've got eyes, and I know what I see when it's staring me in the face."

"He didn't act very interested earlier," Derek muttered.

"So that *is* what you're up to," Lyrica crowed.

"Look, don't say anything to make it more complicated, okay?" Derek said. "Please? He's already not sure of me, and if he thinks I'm talking about him or us behind his back, that's only going to make it worse."

"I won't say a word of what you've said to me," Lyrica promised, "but I won't promise not to say something about anything you do, like the showers. Let me help your campaign along a little."

Derek wasn't sure it would actually be helpful, but he didn't argue. Lyrica would do her own thing anyway.

At the door to the maintenance room, she juggled her keys until she found the right one. "Get what you need," she said. "The plant will probably have to be decommissioned, although Tucker isn't convinced of that yet, so it's not like they're going to need this stuff for regular repairs."

"What will happen to you if it's decommissioned?"

"That doesn't happen overnight. I'll have a job here working with the decommissioning, assuming I want one, for years, probably. There's also units one and two, which should be fine to restart when we have the personnel to do so. I don't know the status of any of my coworkers except Ernesto, who's lying out there in the shed, but from the damage to the buildings, I wouldn't be surprised if others were injured as well. There may be a shortage of qualified people for those two units as well, so I could have a job there if I don't have one or want one here."

"Will it be safe to work there if the radiation here is as high as it was today?" Derek asked, searching through the tools for what he needed.

"That depends on why the radiation was that high, but it will be safe inside the buildings unless this reactor explodes and damages the buildings over there as well," Lyrica said. "The buildings themselves are insulated against radiation."

Derek found a wrench and plumber's tape and went in search of flexible tubing he could attach to the sink faucet rather than having to tear into the wall. "Right, I knew that. But you'd still have to get from your car into the building and back out again."

"Which wouldn't take any longer than it takes you to let Fido out," Lyrica reminded him.. "Your dosimeter isn't yelling at you yet, and as we continue work decommissioning and decontaminating this area, the risk will decrease. My guess is they'll do like they did at Three Mile Island and contain this area more than decontaminating it until the other two units have reached the end of their useful lives. Then they'll do all three reactors together because it's more cost effective that way."

"Aha!" Derek exclaimed, finding a length of heavy plastic tubing. "One shower coming up, first thing in the morning."

"Not tonight?" Lyrica asked with a fake pout.

"It's late, and Sam's asleep already," Derek said. "I don't want to disturb him when he already has a headache."

"Did he check his dosimeter?" Lyrica asked immediately.

"Thank you! He keeps insisting he doesn't need to worry because he isn't nauseated. I didn't check his dosimeter, but he says he did and that the levels aren't high enough to cause headaches yet."

"I'll keep an eye on him for you once you're gone," Lyrica promised.

"Thanks," Derek said, carrying the roll of tubing and the tools out of the room. "I'll look for stuff to make the partitions tomorrow. If I can't find plywood, maybe I can find some lengths of PVC pipe to make frames, and we can drape blankets over them. It'll still be makeshift but better than nothing."

"Definitely better than nothing," Lyrica agreed. "Thank you for doing this. Jeremiah and Thomas are solid nuclear engineers, but I'm not sure either of them has ever picked up a hammer, much less a wrench, and while I know enough to change a light bulb or paint a room, I'm not handy enough to rig a shower or anything like that."

"Then I'm glad I'm here," Derek said, and he was, even if not for that reason.

He left the supplies in the restroom for the night. "I think I'll get some sleep so I can get an early start tomorrow."

"I'm not far behind you," Lyrica said. "I'm just going to see what I can do about getting some of this sweat off me. I'll sleep better if I'm at least a little cleaner."

"Tomorrow night, you can take a shower. I'll stand guard so no one walks in on you."

"I'm looking forward to it already," Lyrica said. "Night, Derek."

"Night, Lyrica."

Derek walked softly into the break room and crossed to where Sambit slept. He gave the room a quick glance, wondering what else he might be able to do to make it more comfortable. If he could find the breakers, he could get into the wiring and add a second switch so they could turn on half the lights at a time instead of having all the lights on or off. That would make it a little easier on the off shift to get some sleep, especially if he could get the partitions built. Sambit snuffled in his sleep, drawing Derek's attention back to him. Derek drew one finger lightly over Sambit's cheek, not nearly as clean-shaven as it had been when they'd arrived, and then stripped down to his T-shirt and boxers to sleep. Everything else could wait until morning.

DEREK started his campaign first thing the next morning, deliberately struggling with the yoga and asking Sambit to help him get his body in the right position several times over the course of their workout. He patted the other man on the shoulder when they were done. "Thanks. That really helped. I have a much better sense of the forms now, instead of feeling like I'm just throwing my arms and legs around every which way."

"You didn't seem to have this much trouble yesterday," Sambit said.

"I think that's because I was so tight yesterday that I couldn't do anything," Derek said. "I'm looser today so I had more range of motion and had to figure out what to do with it."

Sambit looked skeptical, but Derek just smiled and went to eat something before getting started on the plumbing project. He'd rigged a hook from the ceiling to hold the hose and was getting ready to figure out how to attach it to the sink when Tucker came into the restroom. "What are you doing in here? You're supposed to be working on a second robot!"

"Has the second robot arrived yet?" Derek asked, keeping his voice level. Now that he had a reason to stay, he didn't want to get booted out of here any sooner than was already inevitable. "There's only so much I can do without the actual robot, so I thought I'd make a few improvements to make everyone's lives more comfortable in the meantime. Unless you want to live here for months without showering?"

"Does Dr. Johnson know you're doing this?"

"She's the one who let me into the maintenance area so I could get the tools," Derek said. "Now if you don't mind, I'm going to finish up. Let me know when the robot arrives. Until then, I'm going to keep working here."

Tucker scowled but did what he'd come to do and left Derek to work. Sambit wandered in a few minutes later as Derek was measuring the hose for the shower. "There you are. I wondered where you'd gone off to."

"Hi, Sam," Derek said. "Just doing a little home improvement. I might be going home soon if that prick Tucker has his way, but I figured I could make life a little easier for the rest of you."

"Is that really a shower?" Sambit asked.

"Well, a rudimentary one anyway," Derek said. "I don't have anything to use as a showerhead, so it'll just be a stream of water like you'd get out of a garden hose instead of a spray, but it's running water over your head so you can get under it and rinse your hair, your body, whatever. It beats being dirty."

"Does it ever!" Sambit said. "I'm so happy at the thought of actually being clean, I could kiss you."

"You could kiss me anyway," Derek replied, taking a step closer to Sambit. "I wouldn't say no."

"That's not a good idea."

"I think it is," Derek said, advancing another step. Sambit held up his hands as if to ward Derek off, so Derek relented. "It's okay. I'll wait, but I'm going to get my hands on you again before I leave. Consider that fair warning."

"Derek."

"Sambit," Derek replied, mimicking Sambit's exasperated tone. "I know you think I'm fucking around, and I know only time will change your mind, but I'm not yanking your chain or messing with your mind or anything else you might be thinking. This shower is for you. I won't tell anyone else that, but I wouldn't have bothered for their sakes. I'm bothering for yours."

"You don't need to do things on my account," Sambit protested.

"I know I don't need to," Derek said. "I want to, and that's a whole different ballgame. You like football, Sam?"

"Cricket," Sambit replied. "The sport of kings."

"You'll have to explain it to me sometime," Derek said. "I tried watching it once and couldn't follow the game."

"You want to learn about cricket?"

"Sure," Derek said. "You like it, so there must be something to it. It'll give us something in common since you're convinced that is so important."

"You can't possibly be serious," Sambit said.

"As serious as that radiation leak," Derek replied. "But if you don't believe me, that's fine. Give me six months. I'll show you I mean it."

"Six months from now, you won't remember my name," Sambit said.

"Sambit Patel, PhD," Derek said. "I don't know if there's more to it than that because you haven't told me, but I bet I could find out. You work at Texas A&M. They have to have a faculty web site. I'm sure I could find out more there."

"Let it go, Derek," Sambit said. "I don't know why you're so determined to do this, but it isn't worth it."

"Yes, it is," Derek said, "but I won't argue with you anymore. I already figured out I won't convince you that way. Did you need me for something, or were you just wondering where I was?"

"Lyrica said to tell you the next shipment of supplies should be here in about an hour with two more robots and parts for you to get started," Sambit said.

"Then I'd better hurry up and finish in here," Derek replied. "I don't like leaving a job undone."

SAMBIT left the restroom with an insane desire to tear his hair out. Talking to Derek was like talking to a brick wall. Or maybe like a jellyfish. You thought you had him pinned down, and then he twisted out a hole you hadn't even seen. Next time Lyrica could deliver her own message. Sambit was done trying to get anything through Derek's stubborn head. He'd just have to ignore the man for a few more days, and then Derek would be gone, and he wouldn't have to worry about it anymore.

The thought of taking a real shower was appealing, but every time he did, he'd end up thinking of Derek, not at all conducive to a relaxing bath. Of course that was exactly what Derek wanted. He wanted Sambit to think of him. If Sambit had any hope of Derek returning his interest, it might not matter so much, but Derek was leaving. He felt like a broken record, harping on that fact, but it was the wrench in the works, the fly in the ointment, the rain on his parade. As long as Derek was leaving, everything else was pointless because a week at most was not enough time to lay the foundation for a lasting relationship.

"Did you find him?" Lyrica asked.

"He's building a shower."

"Oh, good. He said he was going to work on that."

"Then why didn't you go tell him about the robots yourself?" Sambit asked.

"Because he'd much rather see you than me," Lyrica said.

"Save your matchmaking for someone else," Sambit requested. "It's wasted on me."

"Why is that? I know he's leaving, but you won't be stuck here forever."

"Because when he gets back home, this will just be a bad memory," Sambit replied. "There's no point in starting something with no future."

"I didn't have you pegged as a pessimist," Lyrica said. "You strike me as more positive than that."

"I am," Sambit insisted.

"Then why aren't you grabbing this chance with both hands?" she demanded. "That man in there is gorgeous, smart, caustically funny, and seriously into you. This could be the start of something wonderful. Even if he does leave, there's e-mails, texts, Skype, lots of ways to keep in touch until you get out of here."

"You sound like him."

"That's because we're right. Think about it, Sambit. What do you *really* have to lose?"

It seemed overly simplistic and overly soon to say "his heart" when Sambit had never been one to believe in love at first sight. He had grown up in a culture of arranged marriages and had always believed that a relationship worked successfully because of common backgrounds and common goals, a choice rather than something that one stumbled upon. He believed in lust at first sight, but that was a physical reaction to an attractive stimulus. He wasn't denying Derek was attractive on a physical level. White-blond hair, green eyes, a golden tan, a crooked smile that revealed even white teeth.... There was nothing about Derek that Sambit found unattractive physically, but that wasn't enough. He'd learned that when his first relationship, established on the basis of mutual desire, had fizzled out because they had nothing to say to each other outside of bed.

He and Derek had plenty to say to each other, but Sambit wasn't sure that was an improvement, not when they seemed to argue as much as they talked, and even when they did talk, their conversations only pointed out how different they were. From what Sambit could tell, they shared sufficient intelligence to earn PhDs in their respective fields, and that was about it. While that was a plus in Derek's favor—Sambit had little patience with people who lacked enough intelligence to keep up with him in conversation—it wasn't enough. Different sports, different areas of science, different attitudes on everything from being out to dealing with annoyances, different cities of residence. Sambit didn't know exactly which of Houston's many neighborhoods and suburbs Derek called home, but Sambit had driven out to NASA once. It took over two hours to get there from College Station. They might both be "from the Houston area," but that didn't mean they lived near each other, which further decreased the likelihood of them being able to sustain a relationship after Derek left Bay City.

"My time, my dignity, and maybe a little self-respect," Sambit said, realizing Lyrica was still waiting for an answer, "since I already know how this one ends."

"How does it end?" she asked.

"With a helicopter picking him up in a few days and leaving me behind."

"I'm going to enjoy seeing him prove you wrong," Lyrica declared. "Now, let's see if we can get a better reading from the steam generator. We need conclusive evidence of our theories if we want Tucker to buy into them."

chapter
NINE

"THE shower is ready," Derek said an hour later when he walked into the room where Sambit and Lyrica were working. "It's nothing fancy, but it'll get you clean. I made a sign to put on the door when someone is using it so they don't get interrupted. It's hanging on the paper towel dispenser inside the door. Did anyone think to ask for more paper towels and toilet paper with the supplies?"

"I did," Lyrica said. "They were delivered along with your robots about ten minutes ago."

"Oh, good!" Derek said. "New toys!"

He disappeared before Lyrica could say anything else.

"I swear he's schizophrenic," Sambit said with a shake of his head. "Too many personalities running around inside one body."

"You mean dissociative identity disorder, and he doesn't have that," Lyrica said. "Bipolar, maybe. Probably borderline ADD, but I lived with DID in high school. He doesn't qualify."

"I'm sorry," Sambit said, not knowing what else to say.

"My parents took in foster kids stuck in the system," Lyrica explained. "We had one kid stay with us for a couple of months until it became obvious she needed more psychiatric help than we could give her. She went into a home, and I never did hear what happened to her after that. It was freaky the way you never knew who was going to walk out of her bedroom, but it wasn't just different moods. It was different people. They had different names. All variations on her name, so at first I thought of it as a nickname to fit the mood, but then we realized she didn't remember things that had happened when a different 'person' was in charge. I really hope she got help, because she was a sweet girl, just really, really troubled. Derek isn't like that. And think of it this way. You'll never be bored with him."

"Because I'll never be with him," Sambit said. "Let's get back to work. I want a shower, and the sooner we get this done, the sooner I can take one."

To his relief, Lyrica dropped the matter and turned back to the readings they were analyzing.

Sambit's stomach growling interrupted them two hours later. "I guess we ought to eat lunch," he said, rubbing his noisy belly.

"Probably," Lyrica said. "You find Derek. I'll heat up whatever field rations they sent us this week. That way we aren't all tramping through the break room and disturbing the night shift."

"There's got to be a better solution to that too," Sambit said.

"I know," Lyrica agreed. "If we can get things truly stable, I think it'll be time to clear some offices and closets to make some private sleeping space. Derek was talking about building partitions and working on a switch so we could turn on the lights in half the room at a time instead of all of them coming on, and while that's a very generous offer, it's a temporary solution. I'll think about it over lunch. If nothing else, I can donate my office. It's not very big, but if we moved the desk out, I think we could put two cots in there. Tucker said they were trying to get trailers for us, but there's no guarantee when they'll be able to get trucks in here or how long it will take to get them shielded from radioactivity."

"And in the meantime, we'll keep making do," Sambit said. "Just having the shower will be a huge improvement."

"I agree," Lyrica said. "Go find Derek. I'll bring lunch back in here."

Sambit whistled for Fido, figuring he could see where the dog came from and find Derek that way. Sure enough, Fido stuck his head curiously out the door of one of the larger offices. Sambit walked over to him, stopping at the threshold to look at the chaos inside. Packing was strewn all over the place with circuits and gears and tools in nearly as much disarray. Derek sat on the floor in the middle of it with the carcass of a robot in his lap, the insides torn open as he used a soldering iron on a bit of circuitry. Without looking up, he reached to the side and grabbed another item, adding it to the contraption in his hands. He worked like that for several more minutes, not looking Sambit's way.

Sambit knew Derek was good at what he did. They wouldn't have brought him in otherwise, and with a robot he'd designed and built himself, but watching Derek work showed Sambit a side of the other man he hadn't seen before. All the defense mechanisms were off, all the mood swings were gone, and in their place was a serious, confident, capable man who thought nothing of tearing into a multimillion-dollar robot and gutting it like it was junk so he could add this modification or that one. Having seen Number Five in action, Sambit had no doubt the modifications would be improvements. Perhaps even improvements over Number Five, since Derek was making them with this situation in mind instead of simply because he wanted the robot to be able to do a particular task.

"So is that Number Six?" Sambit asked.

Derek looked up and smiled, the expression so open and full of joy that Sambit thought he might be seeing the real Derek for the first time. "No, and there wasn't a Number One through Four either. It's a film reference. This is… whatever its name is on the box over there."

"You didn't even look?" Sambit asked, amused.

"It didn't matter," Derek said with a shrug. "It was a collection of parts I could plunder to make a robot that can do what we need it to do. I was thinking about it, and if I solder the exterior instead of just fastening it with screws, it would be waterproof and we wouldn't have to stick it in garbage bags every time it went out. We could just hose it down when it came back in."

"What about if you need to get inside to work on it again?"

"I'd have to cut open the solders, but I can do that. It wouldn't be pretty by the time we were done with it, but it would save time in the short run, and that's the real goal, isn't it? To use the robots to get the situation under control enough for people to come in and do their jobs again?"

"That's kind of cold," Sambit said.

Derek shrugged. "I build robots to go on space missions. They're tools that we'll use as long as they're functioning, and then they're space junk. I came to terms with that a long time ago. The Mars rovers have sent back amazing footage and results from the planet's surface, and I'd like to think they still have some usefulness left in them, but they won't ever be coming home. Not in my lifetime anyway. It's rather pointless to get attached."

"I guess so," Sambit said. "You seem to have some affection for Number Five."

"Yes, but it's my robot. I get to take it home with me the same as I do Fido. That's different."

"I suppose," Sambit said, only partially sure he saw the difference. Either way, the robot was Derek's creation. "Lyrica is getting lunch ready if you're hungry."

"Food would be good," Derek said. "I'll have to work on the robot some more this afternoon, but maybe tonight I can start figuring out the wiring in the break room so we can keep half the room dim while the other half has the lights on."

"Lyrica suggested we empty some of the unused offices," Sambit said. "That would provide darkness and privacy."

"I'll move furniture," Derek said. "Just tell me what to move and where to put it."

"We'll have to ask Lyrica," Sambit said, "but we can do that during lunch, maybe."

"Let's eat, then. The sooner we do that, the sooner we can get our work done, and you can take advantage of the new shower."

"It will be nice to be clean."

"And when you're done, I can take advantage of you," Derek added with a wink.

"You're incorrigible," Sambit said with a sigh, ignoring the zing of reaction that went through him.

"No, adorable," Derek said, resting his arm around Sambit's shoulder as they walked toward the control room. "You know I am."

Sambit wanted to argue, but he would have been lying.

"WE'RE done for the day," Lyrica declared a few minutes after seven. "We've been on since seven o'clock this morning. Bad enough that we have to work twelve-hour shifts. We aren't working extra."

"Not in here, anyway," Derek said. "Sambit told me you wanted to clear some offices so people could sleep more easily. If the night shift is coming to work in here, they aren't moving desks."

"We could do it tomorrow," Lyrica said.

"We could," Derek agreed, "but you know what will happen. Tucker will have a list of things for us to do, and we'll get dragged into that, and tomorrow night we'll be having this conversation again. Let's just do it now, or at least do one office. Even if we put all three of our cots in there tonight, it'll be better than having the night shift traipse through our 'bedroom' to get coffee or food."

"I wouldn't complain about a night of uninterrupted sleep," Sambit said. "I haven't had one of those since before the hurricane hit."

"There we go," Derek said. "Decision made."

The look Lyrica sent him spoke volumes about what she thought of his motivations, but Derek ignored it. He didn't have to tell her she was right. Sambit would be more comfortable in the darkness and quiet of an office. Therefore Derek would make it happen.

"So which office can we empty out?" Derek continued when Lyrica didn't immediately give them instructions.

"I guess we'd better start with mine," she said. "I'm not really using it at the moment since I'm in here doing all the work instead of supervising it and writing reports. If it turns out I need my computer for something, we can set it up elsewhere. Even in the break room once that's no longer sleeping quarters."

"Lead the way."

Lyrica showed Derek and Sambit to a small office at the end of the hall opposite the break room. "It's not much," she said, "but it's a start."

Derek looked around the room. The desk took up the majority of the space, with file cabinets against one wall and bookcases on the other one. "Is there anything sensitive in your desk?" he asked. "Anything that would need to stay locked up?"

Lyrica shook her head. "Anything sensitive is either in my computer behind several passwords or it's in the plant manager's office. The master key doesn't even open that office, only his key. We can put my desk wherever and it'll be fine."

"Let's move the computer first," Derek said. "Where do you want it?"

"In the control room, I guess," Lyrica said. "That's where I'm most likely to need it at the moment."

"Sam, you get the monitor and I'll get the CPU. Lyrica, can you get the various cords? You can set it all back up in there while we move furniture, right?"

"Yes, I can set up my own computer," Lyrica said, her voice betraying exasperated good humor. "I'm not helpless or stupid."

"I'm sorry," Derek apologized immediately. "I didn't mean to imply you were, but I work with some brilliant people at NASA who can use a computer to do anything you could possibly want but haven't the slightest idea how to deal with a loose cord. IQ over 150 and not enough common sense to fill a thimble. I stopped assuming people could do something just because they should be able to do it a long time ago."

"Apology accepted," Lyrica said. "Just don't do it again."

They unplugged her computer and moved it into the control room. Derek and Sambit left her to set it back up, and returned to her office. "I think if we pull it out into the hall, we can push it against the wall and it won't block the emergency exit," Derek said. "What do you think?"

Sambit took a rough measure of the desk with his hands and started back out the door into the hallway. Derek moved just enough that Sambit could get by, but not so much that their bodies didn't brush. Sambit shot him a sharp look, but Derek just smiled innocently and shifted so Sambit would have even less space to get back into the office when he was done.

"What are you doing?" Sambit asked, trying to push past Derek.

"Getting close to you," Derek replied, pinning Sambit momentarily. "I'll need a shower when we're done moving furniture. Want to join me?"

"I'll take one when you're done," Sambit said primly.

"Where's the fun in that?" Derek asked. "Come on, Sam. Live a little."

"It's Sambit, and I live plenty. Just because I'm not jumping at the chance to jump you doesn't mean I'm not living."

"I just call it the way I see it," Derek said, stepping back and letting Sambit into the office. His body protested the lack of contact, but he ignored it. He wouldn't gain any ground by pressing the matter now, and if he bided his time, Sambit would get used to his advances and shrug instead of rejecting them. Then he could pounce.

"I think the desk will fit in the hallway," Sambit said, completely ignoring Derek's attempts at flirting.

Derek moved to one side of the desk, lifting it experimentally to see how heavy it was. "There's no way we can move this without taking the drawers out. I can barely lift it, much less carry it."

Sambit nodded and pulled one of the drawers out of the front of the desk. Derek moved right up behind him so that when Sambit stood, he bumped into Derek's chest. Derek grabbed Sambit's hips, steadying him. "If you wanted a hug, all you had to do was say something."

"I didn't—" Sambit bit off whatever he was going to say. "Please move so I can put the drawer in the hallway."

"Your wish is my command," Derek said, grinding his hips against Sambit's ass for a second before stepping back. "I'll get the next drawer."

"I could report you for sexual harassment," Sambit said.

"What are they going to do?" Derek asked, pulling out the next drawer and following Sambit into the hallway. "Fire me? They're already making me leave." He resisted the urge to grope Sambit again as he bent to put the drawer in the corner. Maybe if he'd had both hands free, but as it was, he was afraid he'd spill the contents of the drawer, and then he'd have to deal with Lyrica.

Sambit went back inside and got the third drawer out of the desk before Derek could pin him again, but with his hands engaged with the drawer and unable to swat Derek away, Derek leaned in and pressed a quick kiss to the side of Sambit's neck, unfazed by the smell of several days' sweat. He probably smelled as bad or worse, but they could take a shower as soon as they had the desk and cots arranged.

"Derek!"

"Yes, Sam?"

Sambit huffed and put the drawer in the hallway. "You will not do this to me."

"Do what?" Derek asked innocently.

"Make me want things I can't have," Sambit said "We've discussed this."

"I'm not teasing you," Derek said, his voice completely serious. "I'm trying my damnedest to seduce you, but I am *not* teasing. Yes, I'm leaving. I'm brutally aware of that fact, but you're the one who insists that has to be the end, not me."

"So you want to do what?" Sambit asked, his voice both resigned and curious, a combination Derek would have thought impossible until he heard it in Sambit's tone.

"It's July 15 now," Derek said. "Classes start, what, mid-August? Early September at the latest?"

"Late August," Sambit said. "What's that got to do with anything?"

"That's your real job, not this," Derek reminded him. "By late August, they have to let you go back to College Station because you have students enrolled in your courses who have the right to have you there to teach them. So that's a month. I admit, starting a relationship and then being apart for a month isn't ideal, but it's a month, not six months or a year or some unspecified amount of time that might not ever end. A month. Thirty days, forty-five if they really keep you here until the day before classes start. We can stand to wait thirty days to see each other again if we have to."

"What about the fact that I work at A&M and you work at NASA?" Sambit asked. "They're at least two hours apart."

"So it'll be a bitch of a commute," Derek said with a shrug. "Or I'll figure out a way to work remotely part of the time. Sure, if I'm working on actually building a robot, I have to be there where I can get my hands on the machinery, but a lot of the design and redesign work can be done on any computer. I don't have all the answers, but I don't see that as a reason to walk away without giving us a chance."

"I still say this is a bad idea."

"Because we're so different?" Derek asked.

Sambit nodded.

"You've seen one side of me," Derek said, "and it's not my best one. Give me a chance to show you the rest of who I am. If you don't like that man, if we really are too different, at least we'll know instead of always wondering what could have been. I hate regrets, Sambit, more than I hate almost anything else in the world. I don't want to regret missing a chance with you."

"You're not going to let this go, are you?" Sambit asked.

"No," Derek said. "You can let me have my way now or I can keep trying to persuade you, but I'm not going to give up until you've given me a real chance to prove how good we could be together."

"I'm not just going to let you fuck me," Sambit warned.

"Glad to know that's on the table for later"—Derek grinned—"but I wasn't talking about sex. I already know how good that will be. I was talking about everything else. I'm a hell of a cook."

"How's your sambar?"

"No idea what that is," Derek said, "but let me taste it a couple of times and I'll figure out how to make it."

"Do you even like Indian food?" Sambit asked.

"I love it," Derek replied, "but that doesn't mean I've had every dish out there, or maybe I've had it and not known what I was eating. The menus aren't always in English, some of the places I've gone with my friends. They order, I eat, I pay my part of the bill."

"I'm never going to win an argument with you, am I?" Sambit asked.

"I'll let you win any other argument you want," Derek offered impulsively, "as long as you let me win this one."

"I ought to hold you to that," Sambit said, "but I know you better than that. You'll keep arguing just to keep me in the room with you."

"Would that be such a terrible thing? Being in a room with me?"

"See?" Sambit said. "You just proved my point. Let's move this desk before Lyrica comes down here demanding to know what's taking so long. You will not tell her about this."

Derek grabbed one side of the desk, finding it much easier to lift, and waited for Sambit to pick up the other side. He backed out of the office, admiring the play of muscles beneath Sambit's skin as they carried the desk to its new location. "Cots now?" Derek asked.

"Sure," Sambit said. "Ours, at least. I don't know that we should move Lyrica's without checking with her. You know how women are about people touching their things."

They went back to the break room and gathered the few belongings they'd unpacked. "Jeremiah will be happy not to have to look at your pictures anymore," Sambit said as Derek untacked them carefully from the wall.

"Maybe I should leave them, then," Derek said, cracking a grin in Sambit's direction. "Aren't those born-again guys all about self-mortification?"

"I'm pretty sure that was the medieval Catholic monks," Lyrica said from the doorway. "Take the pictures. They make for pleasant dreams." She looked around the room. "Where's Fido?"

"He was here earlier," Derek said. "I took him outside right after lunch and brought him back in here."

"Don't panic," Sambit said. "Maybe he wandered into the control room with Melanie. He likes her almost as much as he likes you."

"I was just in the control room," Lyrica said. "I didn't see him, although I suppose if he was under one of the desks, I might have missed him."

Derek dropped the pinups on his cot and hurried toward the control room, calling Fido's name as he went. No clatter of claws on linoleum greeted his voice. Entering the control room, he called again.

"Melanie, did Fido come in here with you?"

"No, I haven't seen him since I got up," she said. "He isn't in the break room?"

"No, and he isn't coming when I call him either."

"I'll help you look," she said, getting up from her chair.

"You're supposed to be working, Melanie," Jeremiah called from across the room.

"Don't be a prick, Jeremiah," Melanie snapped. "I won't be gone any longer than if I'd gone to the bathroom."

With Melanie added to their number, they separated and spread out through the main building, calling Fido's name. Finally, in desperation, Derek peered out the door, only to see Fido sitting patiently at the sill. He opened the door and let the dog inside. Fido was sweaty from the heat, panting a little, but otherwise seemed unharmed. "How did you get outside?" he asked the dog, running his hands over the animal's limbs to make sure there were no injuries.

"Oh, good, you found him," Sambit said, coming around the corner. "Where was he?"

"Outside," Derek said, his voice flat. "Last time I checked, he didn't have prehensile toes. Someone let him outside and didn't let him back in."

"That's terrible," Melanie said. "Is he okay?"

"He seems to be, although we'll have to see if he got exposed to enough radiation to be dangerous, but I think it's time for me to finish my work and blow this Popsicle stand. I'm not taking chances with someone being cowardly enough to hurt my dog instead of coming at me."

chapter
TEN

AFTER they found Fido, Derek took the dog with him back to the room where he was working on the robots. Sambit and Lyrica moved their cots and Derek's things as well, in case whoever had let the dog out decided to get at Derek by damaging his belongings. When that was done and Derek had not reappeared, Sambit excused himself to Lyrica and went in search of the man who, an hour ago, had been trying to seduce Sambit into a relationship and now seemed equally determined to flee the scene as fast as possible.

He found Derek much as he'd found him earlier, bent over the robot, but where before he'd seemed lighthearted, having fun as much as working, now he seemed grim, his full concentration on the task at hand. "So you're just going to run away?"

"I'm not running from anything," Derek said, "but I'm not about to let anyone hurt Fido. If they want to come at me head on, fine. I'll fight fair. Coming at my dog isn't fighting fair, and I won't let him be hurt."

"You don't know that it was intentional," Sambit said.

"If it weren't, when I asked, someone would have remembered letting him outside and said something," Derek insisted. "And before you go getting some screwed up thought in your head, this doesn't change a word I said earlier. It just means I might be leaving a little sooner than later."

The words shouldn't have made any difference. Sambit should have been as distrustful of this promise as he had been of everything else Derek had said, but Derek wasn't flirting with him this time. He was angry, ready to leave, and he was still promising to keep in touch with Sambit. Granted, he wasn't angry at Sambit since they hadn't been more than an arm's length apart since lunchtime. Sambit couldn't have been the one to leave Fido outside. Even so, he *was* angry, and Sambit already knew Derek well enough to understand the difference his moods could make in his opinion on matters. "You sounded pretty definite earlier about leaving as fast as possible."

"I am," Derek said, "but I'm not the only one involved in that decision. Tucker has to agree that I've done what the NRC is paying me to do, and someone has to be able to come get me. I have no idea what's going on in Houston as far as recovery efforts, but it's not like the Army is just sitting around with helicopters waiting to come get me as soon as I feel like I've done what I need to do."

"True." Relief swamped him at the thought of having Derek there for a few more days. "You have to teach someone how to operate the robots too. It doesn't do us any good to have them if we can't make them do what we need them to do."

"I'll teach you, and you can teach the others," Derek said. "Or I suppose I can teach you and Lyrica. Right now, I don't want anything to do with the others. I don't know which of them tried to hurt my dog."

"Is he still doing okay?" Sambit asked.

"Well, he hasn't thrown up. I can't ask if he has a headache, but he seems to be acting the same as usual," Derek said. "I'll take him to the vet as soon as I get somewhere that has a vet. Who knows where the one near my house is right now?"

"Are you going to go home?" Sambit asked. "Even with all the damage in the area?"

"Where else would I go?" Derek asked in reply. "The house wasn't damaged. I have a generator and plenty of food stocked up. All my clothes are there, my bike is there. Now that I have a dog, I might have to actually buy a car, God forbid. Even if I don't stay, I have to go back and get what I'd need to be gone for a longer period of time. I didn't have a lot of time to pack before I came here."

"I don't think any of us did," Sambit agreed. "Can I help? I don't know a lot about robots, but I'd be a second pair of hands. Just tell me what to do with them."

"You don't want to make that broad an offer," Derek said, cracking a grin, the first Sambit had seen since they'd realized Fido was missing. "You might not like where I suggest you put them."

"I never said I wouldn't like it," Sambit said. "I said it wasn't wise. Not the same thing at all."

"Well in that case—"

"Still not wise," Sambit interrupted. "Still not playing games."

"I'm not playing games either," Derek promised. "If you want to help, have a seat. You can hold things in place while I solder them."

They worked together for another two hours before the ache in Sambit's back and neck got to be too much.

"I'm sorry," he said. "I have to stop. The headache is coming back, and we have to work another twelve-hour shift tomorrow."

"Go take a shower," Derek suggested. "Even if there's no pounding spray, the heat should help, and being clean will make it easier to sleep. I'm going to work a little longer."

"That's a good idea," Sambit said. "I think I'll try that. Thank you for the shower, in case no one else thinks to say it."

"I only care if you say it," Derek replied with an absent smile, his mind still clearly on his robot.

Sambit shook his head with a soft snort and left Derek to work. He gathered his toiletries from his bag in Lyrica's office, glad he'd thought to toss a towel in along with the couple of changes of clothes. He took his last pair of clean underwear—maybe he should wash out some of his dirty clothes while he was showering—and headed for the restroom Derek had modified. He hung the "showering" sign on the door so people would know he was inside and turned on the water before stripping down.

It wasn't the relaxing spray of water like he had in his shower at home, but it was hot and running and it felt wonderful as it cascaded over his skin. He scrubbed at his scalp, the clean water making him all the more aware of how sweaty he was. He'd wash his hair and then soap it again and let it soak while he washed his body.

He sighed as he rubbed the bar of soap over his skin, feeling the stickiness of too many days without bathing give way beneath the cleansing foam. He arched his back, trying to get every inch of his skin, when a blast of cool air startled him. He spun toward the door to find Derek flipping the lock, something Sambit hadn't bothered to do, and pulling his own shirt off.

"What are you doing here?"

"Getting my hands on you," Derek replied. "You looked like you could use a hand."

Sambit scowled, turning his back on Derek again. He refused to watch the other man undress. It would just make him want things he couldn't have. "I learned how to bathe myself a long time ago."

"That doesn't mean it isn't nice to have help now and then," Derek said, his voice right in Sambit's ear. Sambit froze as Derek took the soap from his hand and ran it over his back. It wasn't all that different from the massage Derek had given him, except this time they were both naked and wet and in a locked room and Derek had been flirting with him all day and....

Sambit groaned as Derek's hands left his back and smoothed their way around to his stomach, pulling him back against Derek's muscled body. He told himself to pull away, but it felt too good to be held. Derek's cock, half hard already, pressed against Sambit's buttocks, and his hands, hard and callused, massaged Sambit's chest as they had once massaged his back. The hair on Derek's chest rubbed against Sambit's back, sensitizing his skin, and he melted, his good intentions disappearing beneath the flood of attraction he'd been fighting since the first time Derek had snapped at him. He'd worry about regretting it tomorrow.

Derek must have sensed his decision because he kissed the patch of skin behind Sambit's ear, the spot that always made him weak in the knees, and whispered, "You won't regret this, I swear."

Sambit didn't know how Derek could realistically keep such a promise, but he'd already decided to leave those concerns for later. Instead he tilted his head to the side, inviting another kiss, and rested his hands on Derek's forearms. Derek rubbed against Sambit more purposefully, making Sambit wish for condoms and lube. He'd had no reason to pack any when he'd gotten the call to come to the plant, and he was sure Derek hadn't thought that far ahead either, but the feeling of Derek's cock rubbing against him, slipping between his thighs to nudge his balls, made him want to say to hell with the dangers. He didn't, of course. He was too practical for that, but it was more proof, if he needed it, of how invested in this his body, at least, had become. With his flirting and teasing touches, Derek had primed Sambit's body for this moment, and now that it was here, he couldn't do anything but tremble and give in.

"Next time," Derek murmured. "Next time we do this, we'll be somewhere we can plan ahead and have everything we need. Tonight, let me make you feel good." As he spoke, one hand moved lower to circle Sambit's shaft, stroking its length slowly and deliberately. Sambit groaned and pushed into the caress, the movement working Derek's cock between Sambit's thighs.

"Yes," Derek said, the sound more hiss than word. "Just like that. It feels good."

"Good," Sambit gasped, squeezing his legs together more tightly, trying to give Derek a narrow space to thrust into. Derek moaned, making Sambit smile. He'd make this good for Derek too, one way or another.

He expected Derek to pick up a fast rhythm of thrusting and stroking. As needy as Sambit was, it was what he would have done if their positions had been reversed, but Derek had other plans, his hand moving leisurely, alternating strokes with tender squeezes. His thumb circled the hooded tip, playing over the foreskin before drawing it back. Sambit gasped when the hot water splashed against the usually veiled skin as Derek's thumb probed the slit, his back arching in need.

"Which part of that did you like?" Derek asked immediately. "If it gets that kind of reaction, I want to do it again."

"Your thumb," Sambit said, his voice husky with desire.

"This?" Derek said, doing it again. Sambit moaned and bucked into his hand. "I'll take that as a yes."

Sambit shook in Derek's arms as he settled in with that simple, powerful touch, mixing whisper-soft brushes of the pad over the sensitive skin with probing passes of the tip through the slit. Sambit's breath sawed in and out of his chest in hoarse little pants that, he hoped, conveyed the depth of his approval to Derek. He wished he could be more eloquent, but between Derek's thumb and his cock still rubbing provocatively against Sambit's balls, words were beyond him.

Derek's other hand, which had been drawing soothing circles on Sambit's stomach as if to hold him in place, moved higher, finding the muscles of Sambit's chest and eventually the nipples at their centers, moving back and forth between them.

It was slow and languid and far more tender than Sambit would have expected from a "fling." Derek peppered little kisses and nips over the side of Sambit's neck and jaw until Sambit finally turned his head, meeting Derek's lips with his own. Even then, they lingered, exploring each other's mouths as Derek explored Sambit's body. Sambit was tempted to turn and return the favor, but that would mean moving out of Derek's embrace and away from the shaft riding between his thighs. He'd take care of Derek before they left the restroom.

Just… later.

Derek broke free from their kiss, biting down on the juncture of Sambit's neck and shoulder, the sudden spike sending erotic shivers through Sambit's body, electrifying every nerve ending. When Derek picked up the pace of his strokes with both his hands and his hips, Sambit trembled and moaned, feeling his climax building deep in his belly. He rocked between the two sources of stimulation. Derek pinched at his nipples, twisting them between his thumb and forefinger, one side, then the other, then back to the first side again until the sensual assault reached a crescendo and Sambit could hold back no longer. He shuddered, his body clenching as he climaxed. Behind him Derek groaned as well, his hips bucking against Sambit's, and Sambit felt sticky fluid coating his thighs.

So much for taking care of Derek later.

Derek nipped at Sambit's shoulder one more time, adding to the aftershocks still zinging through Sambit's system, then licked that little patch of skin beneath his ear again. "Oh, yeah, I'm already looking forward to getting you somewhere horizontal," Derek murmured in Sambit's ear. "If you can do that to me when I'm the one giving you a hand job, I can't wait to see what happens when you get your hands on me."

"I was planning on returning the favor, but you beat me to it," Sambit said.

"That's what you get for being so damn sexy, Sambit. Now give me your soap again because I have a mess to clean up."

The sound of his name, his full name, not that ridiculous nickname, on Derek's lips sent a fresh burst of desire through Sambit. Maybe he'd better stop correcting Derek. Having heard his name that way once in Derek's bedroom voice, he'd be begging every time he heard it again. That might not be any big deal if they only saw each other in the bedroom, but since they had to work together for at least another few days, it probably wasn't a good idea now. He handed Derek the soap but pulled away when Derek reached for him with soapy hands. "That got us into trouble the last time you did that."

"I wouldn't call it trouble," Derek said, stroking a soapy hand over his own cock instead. "I enjoyed it too much for it to be trouble. And so did you, so don't try to deny it."

Sambit bit back the denial that sprang to his lips. Hard to say he hadn't enjoyed it when he'd covered Derek's hand with all the proof he needed of Sambit's enjoyment. Deciding silence was the best option, he took the soap back and washed the stickiness from his inner thighs, wishing as he did that they could have lingered longer in that moment of togetherness. He wasn't a big cuddler by nature, but he enjoyed a little snuggle now and then. He'd bet good money Derek was a snuggler. He put on a fierce front in any situation that might be a threat to him, but Sambit had seen him with Fido. Derek hid a soft heart underneath that prickly exterior, and if he let that guard down, Sambit bet the man lucky enough to see it wouldn't escape Derek's embrace for hours. Then again, if that man had any sense, he wouldn't want to. Sambit repressed a sigh at not getting the chance to be that man, but their current circumstances precluded such intimacies, and he knew better than to think he'd get a chance later. It would simply have to be one of those things he'd regret missing out on.

"You look pensive," Derek said, nuzzling Sambit's neck again.

"I am," Sambit admitted. "That door can't stay locked forever. Eventually we're going to have to put clothes on and go back out there, and when we do, this will be over."

"Not over," Derek said. "On hold for a while, but not over."

Derek's assurance humbled Sambit enough that he nodded. "On hold, then. Either way, I'm not eager for it to happen."

"Neither am I," Derek said, "but I'm not going to let it stop me from enjoying the time we have left. Get some sleep. I'm going to clean up the mess I made working on the robots before I come to bed."

"Lyrica and I moved your cot and pictures," Sambit said, reaching for the towel and starting to dry off. "We didn't want anything to happen to your stuff."

"Thank you." Derek pulled the towel from Sambit's hands and ran it over Sambit's body, whisking away the droplets of water. "How's your head today? I haven't even had time to ask."

"No headache today," Sambit said, stepping away and beginning to dress. "Being clean helps too." He took a deep breath, not entirely sure what he was about to ask was a good idea. "I wouldn't say no to another backrub."

Derek smiled and paused in drying himself. "Let me put my tools away, and I'll see if I can oblige."

chapter
ELEVEN

DEREK sat on the floor of the room where he'd been working on the new robots, Fido lying in the corner again. He sorted through the parts, separating what he still needed to install from what he had ripped out of the insides of the two robot frames.

"I see Sambit isn't the only one who had a shower," Lyrica said from the doorway.

"I installed it for everyone to use," Derek replied, his voice level.

"I wasn't suggesting otherwise," Lyrica replied, "but it must have been a fast shower."

Derek understood what she was hinting at, but he didn't rise to the bait. Not this time. He wasn't a prude, and he hadn't hesitated to share tales of his conquests with friends in the past, but Sambit wasn't a conquest. Sambit was special. "How long do you think it takes to take a shower?"

"Depends on what you're doing in there," Lyrica teased.

"Getting clean," Derek said, hoping to infuse enough finality into his tone that Lyrica would drop the conversation.

"Always a good thing when you've gotten dirty," she agreed. Derek muttered a curse as he felt his cheeks heat, thinking about how exactly he and Sambit had gotten dirty.

"Between the storm and being here, it's been five days since I had a shower," Derek replied, hoping he hadn't given them away. He didn't think she'd have a problem with it, but it was still too new and precious to share with anyone else.

"Uh-huh," Lyrica said. "Did Sambit tell you we moved your cot and bag?"

"He mentioned it when I saw him earlier," Derek said. "I appreciate it, but I want to finish up in here so I'll be able to get a good start with the rest of the modifications in the morning. I'll be in later."

"Don't rush on my account," Lyrica said. "I pushed aside a desk in another office and moved my cot in there because there wasn't really enough room in my office for all three of us. For the cots, yes, but not really for three bodies on top of them."

"I don't want to wake Sambit up when I come in either," Derek said. "Does he know you're sleeping elsewhere?"

"I told him when I saw him just now," Lyrica replied. "I'll let you finish your work. Enjoy your night."

"I'm sure I'll sleep very well," Derek said neutrally, even as he imagined all the other ways he could have an enjoyable night alone in a locked office with the man he was falling for far too rapidly for his own good. He wouldn't do any of those things because that wasn't the way he wanted to start a relationship with Sambit, their interlude in the shower notwithstanding. He could follow through on his offer to give Sambit another massage, though, and show Sambit that he was as capable of restraint as he was of action. He put away the last of his tools and supplies. "Good night, Lyrica."

Lyrica smiled and walked down the hall away from the office Derek had helped clear an hour earlier. Derek went in the opposite direction, heart pounding as he approached the office where Sambit would be waiting. They wouldn't *really* be sleeping together, with the two separate cots and no real way to make a single bed, but it would be just the two of them in the room, a far more intimate situation. It was, in complete innocence, more than he had shared with most of his past lovers. An only child, he'd never had to share his space with anyone else until he got to college. He'd run off two roommates his freshman year and had moved off campus after that rather than have to deal with anyone else. Since then, he'd occasionally let a lover spend the night or, slightly more frequently, had spent the night at a lover's house, but he'd never invited anyone to move in with him or accepted such an invitation from anyone else. He liked his solitude, and he liked having everything in its own place. Having other people around complicated that because no one seemed capable of respecting those places. Sambit hadn't bothered any of Derek's belongings since they'd been here except to move them this evening. While that might have bothered Derek under different circumstances, at the moment he could only be grateful. He reached the office, still wondering how to explain the crazy thoughts running through his head to Sambit, but Sambit had fallen asleep waiting for him, his soft breathing the only sound in the darkened room.

Derek stripped down to his underwear now that Lyrica was sleeping in another room and lay down on his own cot, patting Fido's head a few times when the dog whined at his side. "I know, boy," he said. "You're having a hard time here. I am too, but I think we'll be going home soon. You'll have to help me get my house fixed up because I'm actually thinking about inviting someone over. We can move some of the robotics stuff out to the garage and clear out one of the upstairs bedrooms so he has an office of his own. Think he'd like that, Fido?"

Fido licked Derek's hand, circled around a couple of times, and lay down beneath Derek's cot, leaving Derek alone with his thoughts and his planning. He was getting ahead of himself, thinking about rearranging his house to make room for Sambit when Sambit didn't even believe Derek would be interested in him once he left. Derek didn't know how things would work out, but for once, he was willing to fight for their future rather than write off the relationship because it would require more work than he was willing to put into it. Sambit had touched something inside him that no one had ever managed to do, tripping Derek's protective instincts while being more than capable of taking care of himself. Derek had known men who appealed to his protective side, but their general helplessness, real or feigned, got on his nerves before long. He had also known men who were disgustingly capable and appealed to his desire for an equal, but their refusal to accept his occasional need to look out for his lover had driven him away. Sambit appealed to both sides, refusing to back down from Derek in an argument but willing to bend when Derek got protective over his headaches.

Now he simply had to convince Sambit to believe him.

He hoped his attentions in the shower had helped rather than hurt. Sambit hadn't pulled away, which was a good first start, and he'd certainly seemed to enjoy their interlude as much as Derek had if the mess on his hand had been any indication. Even more than that, the way Sambit had leaned against Derek so trustingly, as if he knew Derek would not let him fall, made Derek hope Sambit was beginning to believe Derek's promises. Derek certainly intended to keep them because he couldn't remember the last time he'd had such an explosive round of sex, and that was just a hand job and a bit of frottage. The mere memory of thrusting through the channel formed by Sambit's thighs made Derek's body react again. He couldn't even imagine what it would feel like if Sambit ever returned the favor.

Derek rolled to his side, peering through the near darkness at the outline of Sambit's body on the nearby cot. The man wasn't classically handsome, but everything about him pulled at Derek on a visceral level. His dark skin contrasted with Derek's paler coloring, the juxtaposition drawing Derek's attention again and again as they touched. Sambit had more of a swimmer's build than the muscular bodies Derek tended to fantasize over when he was between lovers, but Derek had seen the strength in the lithe muscles as they practiced yoga. Sambit might not be muscle-bound, but he was strong and fit in probably a healthier way than the pinups Derek admired. More than that, he had been warm and responsive beneath Derek's hands, making Derek's senses spin with heady desire. Derek could still feel the friction of Sambit's body hair against his erection as he moved between the other man's legs, a different sensation than sliding into a hot piece of ass both because of the coating of hair and because of not needing a condom. The frottage against bare skin had been unbelievably erotic, enough to make Derek want to try it again to see if the magnitude of sensation would continue over time. If it did, that could quickly become a favorite way to make love.

The choice of words, even in the silence of his thoughts, drew him up short. He didn't think in those terms. He never had. If he needed to be polite, he talked about having sex, but usually he was perfectly content to call a fuck a fuck. So why couldn't he bring himself to dismiss this encounter the same way?

There was no easy answer to that question, and the frustration of not being able to pin down his feelings followed him into sleep.

DEREK almost refused when Sambit woke him up to do yoga, the need to finish the robots and start testing them combining with the vague memory of troublesome dreams to leave him feeling unsettled and grouchy, but he stopped the refusal before it formed. The robots could wait an hour while he learned a little more of what Sambit could teach him about yoga and about controlling himself. Maybe the yoga would even help him find his balance again after the night of fitful sleep, and if it didn't, at least he'd know he'd tried. To that end, he really focused on the breathing exercises Sambit had him do before they started, drawing in energy from around them as he inhaled and forcing out negativity with each exhale. By the time they started the Salute to the Sun, Derek could already feel the stress starting to fade.

When they had worked out for half an hour and Derek had taken care of Fido, he sat down to tinker with the robots and marveled that despite the inherent stress of the situation, he felt calmer and more in control of himself than he had in a long time. "Maybe there is something to this yoga thing," he said to Fido as he worked. "Think Sambit would be willing to keep teaching me? He'd have to get up a little earlier if we're going to do yoga before I leave to drive to Clear Lake if he expects me to stay in College Station with him."

Fido didn't even look up from where he napped in the corner. Derek shook his head indulgently and went back to work. When he looked up again, several hours had passed and Sambit stood in the doorway, his quiet cough drawing Derek's attention. "Are you getting sick?" Derek asked immediately.

"No, I just didn't want to startle you," Sambit said. "I came to see how you were doing on the new robots and whether you'd be willing to take Number Five out again if the new ones weren't ready."

"I've got one ready to test," Derek said, "although I'm not ready to declare it finished yet. We can give it a shakedown run, though. You can start learning how to control it since I'll have to teach someone before Tucker makes me leave, and I'd rather teach you than have to work with any of the night crew."

"So you'll just make me work with them instead," Sambit said with a grin.

"Or you can be the only robot operator and they can just monitor the situation at night," Derek replied. "I don't care if you don't teach any of them how to control the robots."

"Melanie isn't that bad," Sambit said. "You could teach her."

Derek shrugged. "We'll see. Here, take this. The joystick is just like you'd expect. Forward, backward, left, and right. Let's get it to the control room and hook up the cameras to one of the computers there, and then we can start working on the other controls and things like getting it to climb stairs."

Sambit took the controller and guided the robot to the control room without any problem. "See, it's easy," Derek said.

"Somehow I doubt it'll stay that easy when it's uneven ground or stairs or other obstacles, but I suppose it's a good start."

"You have to start somewhere," Derek agreed, handing Sambit the other controller that moved the robot's arms and activated the various sensors. "Now play around with that one while I install the interface."

"What are you doing?" Lyrica asked, coming over to where they were working.

"You'll need the robots to interact with a computer besides mine," Derek said. "I'll need admin approval to install the interface on this computer, unless there's another you'd rather I use."

"I'll put my password in when it asks for it," Lyrica said. "This one is as good as any other."

Derek finished installing the software and turned back to Sambit. "Getting the hang of it?"

"Not really," Sambit said, "but I suppose practice is the only way to get better."

"That's right," Derek agreed with a wink. "Lots of up close and personal practice."

He could have sworn Sambit's dark skin darkened even more as his eyes darted toward Lyrica. If she thought anything of Derek's comment, she gave no indication, continuing with her work as if the men weren't even there.

"Sorry," Derek said, lowering his voice. "I didn't mean to embarrass you."

"It's not that," Sambit said, "but it's none of their business, and I prefer to keep my private life private. I'm not ashamed of what we did, before you get that idea in your head, but I wasn't raised to talk about certain things. I can't be that casual about it."

"I wasn't being casual," Derek assured him. "I was going more for flirtatious, but I obviously blew that one."

"Just not around anyone else, okay? I have to work with them after you leave, and I'd rather keep things on a professional footing as much as possible."

"Okay." It went against Derek's nature to curb his tongue or his actions simply because someone else might not approve, but Sambit had asked so Derek would do his best to follow through, another sign of how deeply Sambit had wormed his way into Derek's esteem. He'd ended relationships in the past because the man had asked Derek to change. It made Derek's willingness to bend now that much more baffling.

He put the thought aside for later. He needed to concentrate on the robot now.

"HOW much longer before those robots are ready?"

Derek looked up from where he was working to see Tucker standing in the doorway, a much less welcome sight than Sambit's interruptions always were.

"I tested the first one this afternoon," Derek replied. "It needs a few more adjustments, but it should be ready to go by tomorrow. I haven't gotten the second one ready to test yet because I wanted to see what worked and what didn't on the first one."

"Well, get busy," Tucker snapped. "I want them both operational by the day after tomorrow. There's a supply convoy coming at noon, and you're leaving with it."

"I'll do my best," Derek said, "but even I can only work so many miracles without a break."

"I thought you were supposed to be the best NASA had to offer," Tucker sneered.

"There's a robot rebuilt from the chassis out," Derek pointed out. "I'd say that's pretty damn good for two days. If you want the other one done, go away and let me work."

Tucker scowled but left as Derek had demanded. Derek took a deep breath, using the techniques Sambit had taught him to breathe out his temper rather than throwing something at Tucker's back.

"You all right?" Sambit asked. "I saw Tucker storming out."

"He's decided I'm leaving on the next supply convoy," Derek said, "so I have a day and a half to get the robots ready to go and teach you how to operate them. I don't think I'll be getting a lot of sleep."

"Let me tell Lyrica and I'll be back to help," Sambit offered. "I can follow directions even if you still have to figure out what to tell me to do."

"You sure?" Derek asked. "This isn't your job."

"Maybe not, but it'll benefit me as much as anyone else if it's done right rather than rushed because Tucker didn't give you enough time to finish. I'll be right back."

Derek looked over at Fido lying in the corner and then back at the robot. He couldn't stay, not with Tucker determined to get rid of him and someone willing to hurt his dog to get to him, but he could spend the next thirty-six hours giving Sambit a crash course in robotics.

BY THE time exhaustion led Sambit to call it quits for the night, his head was spinning with all the information Derek had imparted in the ten hours since he had offered to help. The biggest surprise hadn't been how much Sambit had to learn but how good Derek was at explaining it all in terms Sambit could relate to. Granted, he was himself a highly intelligent man with a PhD in nuclear physics, but there was only so much overlap in the two fields. Sambit never felt like Derek was talking down to him, but at the same time, he hadn't been lost in the vernacular, picking up the rationale behind the choices Derek made for the robots, giving each of them special features rather than trying to make both of them capable of everything they might need to be able to do. Sambit wasn't an expert yet, but he wasn't nearly as overwhelmed by the thought of operating the robots and maybe even maintaining them without Derek as he had been earlier in the day.

He stretched his arms above his head, arching his back.

"Keep doing that and I'll get ideas."

Sambit spun at the sound of Derek's voice. "I'm too worn out to do anything but sleep."

"I bet I could convince you otherwise."

"You probably could," Sambit admitted, "but that doesn't make it a good idea. I'm tired and my back hurts and I'm fighting another headache. I need a good night's sleep because tomorrow we have to test what we did today, and you have to show me how to make any changes that need to be made because I'll have to keep tweaking them after you leave."

"Say the word and I'll fight leaving," Derek offered.

"What about Fido?" Sambit asked. The dog lifted his head at hearing his name, but when Sambit made no effort to call him over, he put his head back down and settled for wagging his tail.

"We keep him with us at all times," Derek said. "It's not ideal, but it's never been ideal. All you have to do is ask, and I'll stay."

And postpone the inevitable.

"If I get in over my head with the robots, can I send you an e-mail for help?"

"E-mail, text, call, or anything else," Derek offered immediately. "Get your phone. I'll program all the numbers in."

Sambit unclipped his phone from his belt and handed it to Derek. Derek tapped on the keypad for several minutes, including punching the call button so Sambit's number would show up on his own call record, before handing the phone back to Sambit. "There. All the ways you could possibly need to get in touch with me. I put my home, cell, and work numbers in there as well as my personal and work e-mails. Obviously I'd rather you only use the work number and e-mail for robotics stuff rather than personal conversation, but you can call or text my cell anytime you want. I don't know how long it'll be before Kenneth expects me back at work at NASA, but if it's not a convenient time to talk, I can always choose not to take the call."

"You don't really want me calling just because," Sambit demurred, "but thank you for the numbers. If we have an emergency, it will help to be able to reach you."

Derek grabbed his shoulders, shaking him lightly. "If you don't want to call or text, that's your choice. I'll be disappointed, but I'll live with it, but don't put words in my mouth. You can put other things there all you want and I'll happily suck on them all night long, but I meant what I said about wanting to hear from you."

"Everything goes back to sex with you, doesn't it?" Sambit asked, the off-color comment rubbing him the wrong way. "I'm going to bed."

"Why are you so determined to avoid me?" Derek demanded. "I don't know how many more ways I can try to prove to you that I'm serious."

"You can't," Sambit said. "Two days, four days, a week, that's not long enough to prove anything, especially under extenuating circumstances like these. If we'd met at a conference or even at a bar, maybe things would be different, but we're thrown together here day in and day out, and there's nothing normal about that."

"Fine," Derek said. "I'll leave with the supply convoy, but you aren't getting rid of me that easily. I won't disturb you during the day because I know you have to work, but I expect to hear from you every evening. I'm still not convinced your headaches are just headaches. If nothing else, I want to know what your dosimeter reading is so I know you haven't been overexposed to radiation. I may not be here, but that won't stop me from caring about what happens to you, and it won't stop me from wanting to be with you as soon as you're out of here."

"We'll see," Sambit said. "I'm not saying you're wrong. I'm just not convinced you're right, and the only way to prove either one of us right is to let time pass and see what happens."

"Fair enough," Derek said, "but I'm not going to stop trying to convince you. Think you can deal with that for the next fifty years or so?"

He was probably stubborn enough to do it, too, Sambit thought. "You'll do what you want no matter what I say so I'm not going to argue with you. I was serious about being tired, though, so I *am* going to bed now."

"Make yourself comfortable, and I'll rub your shoulders for you again."

"It's not that kind of headache this time," Sambit said. "It's above my eyes and in my temples. A backrub won't help that."

"So I'll try something else," Derek said. "Lie down. I'll be right back."

Sambit rolled his eyes. Derek needed to learn the meaning of the word "no." With a sigh, he took off his shirt. He'd take a shower in the morning after he did his yoga. As much as he needed one, he was too tired to shower tonight. He debated leaving his trousers on, but he'd be more comfortable without them so he stripped down to his briefs and climbed under the covers quickly. He didn't need to give Derek another excuse to jump him again, not that he could honestly complain about the results last time.

"Leave your eyes closed," Derek's voice said above him. "I'm just going to put this cloth on your forehead. The heat and steam should help with the pressure."

Before Sambit could decide how to respond, Derek had laid a warm, wet cloth across his eyes and forehead. The heat did feel good, and Sambit felt the pressure in his sinuses loosening somewhat. Then Derek's fingers settled on his temples, rubbing in deliberate circles, the pressure just this side of painful. "Relax," Derek said softly. "I know it feels too hard now, but give it a minute and it'll help the pain."

"How do you know?"

"I used to do this for my mom when she got really bad headaches around her eyes. She always said it was the only thing that made her feel better."

It was one more instance of the soft, fiercely protective heart beneath the prickly surface. Sambit gave up fighting and relaxed into Derek's care. It wouldn't be such a terrible thing to be on the receiving end of that protectiveness now and then as long as Derek didn't smother him with it when he didn't need it. He hadn't so far. He'd worked alongside Sambit as an equal until Sambit showed signs of distress. Only then had the protectiveness kicked in. Sambit could think of worse qualities to have in a partner.

The thought startled him enough to open his eyes.

"Close your eyes," Derek scolded. "You're supposed to fall asleep while I'm doing this so you'll feel better in the morning."

Sambit did as he was directed, his thoughts racing. He'd been deliberately avoiding any thought of a future with Derek beyond the few days they'd been together at the power plant, but his heart had other ideas. He knew this was a bad idea, but he couldn't seem to stop himself. It would get easier once Derek left, he hoped, because while Sambit couldn't deny his own investment in the situation any longer, his assessment of the chances of making things work between them hadn't changed. He wouldn't do anything to deliberately sabotage their relationship, but he still believed it wouldn't last more than a week or two beyond Derek's departure.

Derek moved the cloth from Sambit's forehead, his fingers massaging above Sambit's eyebrows, digging in slightly as they had done at his temples. As before, any harder and it would have hurt, but Derek always stayed one step shy of that point, and Sambit felt the pressure behind his skull lessen bit by bit.

He reached up and squeezed Derek's wrist. "Thank you. That helped."

Derek lifted Sambit's hand to his lips, kissing the palm gently. "Good. Now go to sleep."

Sambit almost asked how he was supposed to do that with Derek distracting him, but the touch on his face gentled, soothing him into sleep.

chapter
TWELVE

"I'LL call tonight to see how things went with the robot," Derek said as he packed his bag and folded up his cot. They still had a few hours before the supply convoy arrived and Derek had to leave, but he wanted to spend as many of those hours as possible working so he figured he'd better pack now while he had a chance. He didn't want anything to get left behind because Tucker threw him out the door when the supply convoy was ready to leave.

"I'm sure they'll be fine," Sambit said from where he sat on his cot nearby. "We tested them yesterday and they worked great."

"Yes, but that was under test conditions. When you get them out in the reactors and exposed to the radiation, they might not perform as well. It's a tricky business, robotics. Besides, I want to know if you're having more headaches. I don't like that."

"I know you don't, but my dosimeter isn't anywhere near a dangerous dose, and I still don't have any other symptoms," Sambit reminded him. "It's stress, not radiation, because if it were radiation poisoning, I wouldn't feel better in the morning or after your massages."

"I hate that I'm leaving you here," Derek said, closing his bag and sitting down next to Sambit. "I feel like I'm abandoning you and Lyrica. I know it wasn't my idea, but even so, it feels wrong."

"I know you'd stay if Tucker would let you," Sambit said, squeezing Derek's hand. "Go home and get your house fixed back up. I know you said you didn't have any flooding, but you should still check things out to make sure there wasn't other damage. They grabbed us and brought us here so quickly after the storm passed that I'm sure you didn't have a chance to check things out thoroughly."

"No, I didn't," Derek admitted, "but I didn't see anything obvious before I left. I have to get stuff for Fido too. I don't exactly have dog supplies at my house. I took some food from the house I found him in, figuring that would hold me until I could find an open store with something in stock. Who knows what I'll find when I get back? I'm pretty sure I was the only one in the neighborhood who rode out the storm. When the others come back and see the decimation, they may not decide to rebuild. It happened a lot after Katrina in New Orleans. People found it easier simply to move than to start over where they had been before."

"See?" Sambit said. "You'll be so busy with the rebuilding going on around you that you won't have time for me. And you'll have to get back into your real job as soon as you can too. I don't imagine NASA can afford to shut down for long."

"They can't," Derek said. "That's one of the reasons they have different installations, so that if one goes offline for something, the others can take up the slack temporarily. It won't be long before my office is back up and running, though. They have contingency plans in place for every disaster imaginable, including that bitch of a storm." He saw Sambit's flinch and could have kicked himself. "Sorry. I'm trying to watch my language. I know it's a bad habit."

"You've done a lot better since the first day," Sambit said, "and I appreciate it. Even if I still react when it slips out. You don't have to change on my account, you know."

"Sure I do," Derek said, leaning over to kiss Sambit lightly. "You won't stay with me if I'm constantly making you uncomfortable with my cussing."

"You won't be around after today."

"For a few weeks." Derek refused to let Sambit get in the mindset of his departure meaning the end of their relationship. "Then you'll be back on campus and we'll be able to see each other more often. Hell— heck, I might even move to College Station if you ask me nicely enough."

Derek could see Sambit's skepticism on his face but let it go. Only time and carrying through on his promises would convince Sambit of his sincerity. "Let's go finish our tests," he said instead. "I don't want to give Tucker any reason to snipe at you after I'm gone because I didn't think of something before I left."

"If there's a problem, I'll call," Sambit said. "Really. I'm not going to pretend to be an expert at something I'm not."

"Two of a kind beats a straight any day," Derek said. "We'll show Tucker what we're made of, even if I have to do it from a distance."

Sambit chuckled. "Two of a kind, huh?"

Derek shrugged. "We are, aren't we? Two gay men, two PhDs in a world that values athleticism more than intelligence, two outsiders trying to make our way in a world that doesn't always understand us. Maybe the reasons we're outsiders are different since you're less open about your sexuality than I am, but you said yourself that being Indian sets you apart sometimes."

"I guess we do have a few things in common, when you put it that way," Sambit said.

"I told you we did." Derek resisted the urge to crow more than that or to push for more of a commitment than Sambit was willing to give at the moment. He'd stick to his plan and let time and determination win the other man over. "Let's go. I heard Tucker's bellow, and I don't want to give him a reason to yell at you once I'm gone."

EVERYTHING seemed quieter after Derek left, and not in a good way. Sambit had gotten used to having him around, to the shimmer of nerves that accompanied his presence, to the way he seemed to dominate a room, drawing attention to himself even when he was working and not doing anything to actually demand that attention.

All the confidence he had felt with the robots while Derek was at his side faded as he sat down at the computer to send the robot out to check on the turbines again. The uneven ground would add complications he wasn't comfortable dealing with.

Two of a kind beats a straight. Derek's words echoed in Sambit's head, making him smile. He might be the only one sitting here, but Derek was only a call or a text away if Sambit got into a situation he couldn't handle on his own.

"It's quiet with Derek gone," Lyrica said, sitting down next to him and peering over his shoulder. "Let's see what's going on with that turbine, shall we?"

Sambit guided the robot around the control building toward the breach in the secondary containment structure where they could access the compromised turbine and pipes. Their hope was that as they had continued to pump boron into the reactor, they would have decreased the radioactivity of the entire complex, but this was their first opportunity to test the results of their experiment. Until they could get the radioactivity under control, it wouldn't be safe to begin repairs on the containment structure or to start decommissioning the reactor.

He had just reached the edge of the containment structure when his phone buzzed on his belt. Frowning, he brought the robot to a stop and pulled out the phone.

Don't forget to compensate for the changing center of balance when you go up or down an incline. Miss you already.

Sambit smiled. *Thanks for the reminder. I needed it.*

"Sorry about that," he said to Lyrica. "Let's see if we can get this guy inside. I'm not Derek, but he taught me a thing or two while he was here."

His phone buzzed again, but he ignored it this time. It was probably Derek chiding him for not saying he missed Derek too. He did miss the other man, but he didn't need to encourage him. He was incorrigible enough as it was. Instead he focused on adjusting the position of the robot's various appendages to keep the center of balance in the right place as the robot moved.

"You're pretty good at this," Lyrica said. "I'm impressed."

"Derek's a good teacher."

"Does A&M need a robotics professor?" Lyrica teased.

"Even if they did, Derek would be crazy to leave NASA to teach robotics instead of working on the cutting edge of the field," Sambit said with a shake of his head.

His phone buzzed again.

"Answer him," Lyrica said. "He's going to keep texting you until you do."

Sambit scowled at her as he pulled his phone out again.

You didn't say you miss me too.

He scrolled down to the second text.

You do miss me, don't you?

"Go on, tell him you miss him," Lyrica prodded.

"How do you know I miss him?" Sambit asked.

"Believe me, I know," Lyrica insisted.

"Fine," Sambit said with a huff. *Yes, I miss you, but don't let it go to your head. I miss Fido more.*

Bastard. Just for that I won't send you a picture of him in his new house when we get there.

"You shouldn't bait him," Lyrica said over his shoulder. "He might decide not to help us."

"Are you reading my texts?" Sambit demanded. "Some things are private."

"You flirting with Derek? Please. You two couldn't have been any more obvious."

"What do you mean?" Sambit asked warily.

"You're attracted to him, he's attracted to you," Lyrica said. "You're both unattached as far as I know. There's no harm in acting on that attraction."

"We didn't—that is—"

"Methinks you doth protest too much," Lyrica interrupted.

"That isn't how the quote goes," Sambit corrected automatically.

"Not the point," Lyrica said. "I don't care if you flirt with him. I think it's great that something positive could come out of this snafu. Just don't let Tucker catch you doing it."

"You're the one who told me to text him back!"

"I didn't say don't text him back. I didn't even say don't text him when Tucker's around because you've got plenty of valid reasons to text him. I said don't let Tucker catch you flirting. Your smile reading those texts would have given you away for sure if he'd been in here. Nobody smiles that way while they're working."

"What way?" Sambit asked.

"Half charmed, half annoyed, and totally in love."

"I'm not in love with him," Sambit insisted. He couldn't be. He'd only known Derek a week. There was no way he could fall in love in that timeframe, even with the extenuating circumstances.

"Mmmhmm," Lyrica said. "Think what you want. Now, if you're done flirting with your boyfriend, we have work to do."

Sambit huffed softly and turned his attention back to the computer screen. Lyrica was full of it. There was no other explanation. He wasn't even sure he liked Derek half the time. He was *not* in love with the man.

He managed to keep the robot from flipping over as it worked its way into the secondary containment area. The readings on the Geiger counter were definitely lower than they had been when Derek had taken Number Five into the area, but they were still higher than they should have been.

"So what now?" Sambit asked.

"I guess it depends on whether we look at this as proof that the boron solution is working or whether we look at it as proof that we still have a problem."

"Assuming our deductions about the cause of the radioactivity are correct, we'll always have a problem," Sambit said. "The issue is controlling the symptoms of the problem sufficiently that we can get people in there to decommission the reactor, and these readings suggest we're doing that successfully."

"So let's present them to Tucker and see what he'll authorize us to do next."

SAMBIT'S last text left a smile on Derek's face that lasted until the Army Humvee reached Houston and headed south toward Pearland. Derek had seen enough on the helicopter ride into Bay City to know the damage was significant, but he'd been so focused on the situation at the power plant that he hadn't dwelled on it. Now he had no choice but to face the utter devastation wrought by the storm. Only one house in three appeared unscathed, but he'd seen enough flooding to know that many of them could have foundation damage that wouldn't be visible to the naked eye. As they drove down Highway 288, the destruction got even worse, entire groups of homes flattened by the storm. He was sick to his stomach by the time they turned off at Broadway and worked their way deeper into town. The floodwaters had receded, but he saw little sign of life beyond that. Debris littered the usually immaculate streets; the manicured trees and shrubs were missing limbs or torn up by their roots. The brick walls around the exteriors of the neighborhoods seemed to have held up fairly well, but the roofs on the houses inside the walls were missing more often than not. Overlying it all was the stench of decay.

"You sure you don't want me to take you somewhere else?" the soldier driving the vehicle asked. "I don't know how safe it would even be for you to stay here."

"I don't have anywhere else to go," Derek said. "My family is all the way up by Texarkana, and I can't get the dog there on my bike. I'll be fine. I stocked up to weather the storm, and there's no way the city's just going to die because of this. People will come back, and it'll get better. Just like New Orleans after Katrina hit. It took time and a lot of work, but it'll happen here too."

"If you're sure," the man said, sounding skeptical still. "I've got orders to take you wherever you want to go, so if this is where you want to be, I'm not going to argue."

"It's just around the corner," Derek said, pointing to the street that led into his neighborhood.

His subdivision seemed slightly less beaten up than the areas closer to the freeway, but that could have been wishful thinking. The soldier stopped in front of Derek's house, easily identifiable by the fact that it wasn't falling down. "Do you need a hand with your gear?"

"No, but thank you," Derek said, climbing out of the truck and helping Fido down. He shook the soldier's hand. "I appreciate the lift."

"I'm going to let the National Guard unit in the area know you're here," the soldier said. "They can come by and check on you periodically, make sure you have everything you need and that no one's bothering you and all."

"Thanks," Derek said one more time before whistling for Fido, who was sniffing his way around the yard. "Yes, I know, boy. It stinks."

The humidity had to be at ninety-eight percent again and the temperature well over ninety given the way he was already sweating, even with the wind from the open windows in the Humvee. The stench from the floodwaters and the rotting vegetation was nearly overwhelming. He only hoped his generator was still running because if his house smelled this bad, he was going to have to figure out how to hold Fido and ride his motorcycle at the same time.

"Let's go inside, okay? It'll be better there."

Fido followed him up the sidewalk, the concrete slabs that had been underwater out of place because of the dirt shifting underneath them. "The fucking HOA is going to make me replace the entire sidewalk, aren't they?" he asked the dog. "I guess that's better than having to replace the entire house."

The interior of the house was blissfully cool and odor-free when Derek opened the back door and let himself and Fido inside. He stroked the dog's ears a few times, then pulled out his phone again.

I made it home safe. It's even worse than I thought. Can I come live in College Station?

He hit Send and went into the kitchen to find a bowl for Fido. Sambit would reply or not eventually, but in the meantime, Derek had other things he had to take care of.

Half an hour later, as Derek was climbing out of the shower, his phone beeped to indicate he'd received a text.

I have a spare bedroom, but it's full of boxes. It's yours if you clear it out.

Who are you and what have you done with my Sam?

Sambit's reply thrilled Derek, but it was out of character, making him fear the answer was in jest rather than serious. Then there was the matter of living in the spare bedroom instead of sharing Sambit's room, but he figured that would last all of about ten minutes.

It's Sambit, not Sam, and I'm not yours.

That's my Sam, stubborn to the end. What does your dosimeter say?

It took a few minutes before Sambit replied.

.25. The same as yesterday.

Derek frowned at the phone for a moment. *Send me a picture of it*

What?

You heard me. Send me a picture of the dosimeter reading.

A few minutes later, a picture showed up on his phone with a .25 Gy reading on the dosimeter. All he could see was the readout, though. He flipped through his contacts and texted Lyrica. *What is Sam's dosimeter reading?*

.25. Do you not trust your own boyfriend?

Not where that's concerned. Does he have a headache?

Why are you asking Lyrica questions about me? Ask me if you want the answers.

Then tell me the truth, Derek texted back.

I told you AND I sent the picture. What else do you want?

Derek wanted Sambit there with him safely away from the power plant, or if he couldn't have that, then he at least wanted Sambit in College Station. Since he could have neither of those for the moment, he settled for texting back. *Does your head hurt tonight?*

No, you left. There's no one around to give me a headache.

That's cold, Sam. That's really cold.

Sambit didn't reply for several minutes.

I'm sorry. That was inappropriate. Yes, my head hurts. I wish you were here. I'd take a backrub tonight.

Take a hot shower instead and think of me. I built it for you.

Sambit didn't reply to that, but Derek didn't really expect him to. Sambit had pretty much always backed away from any kind of declaration. Derek could let it go for now. He couldn't do anything other than text or e-mail, or maybe call occasionally, until Sambit made it out of there anyway.

He let Fido out so he could explore the backyard and dug through the cabinets for something for dinner.

chapter
THIRTEEN

DEREK made it almost to lunch the next day before the need to touch base with Sambit became overwhelming. He grabbed his phone, intending to send off a witty, flirtatious text, but he stopped before he did more than program Sambit's number as the text recipient. He wasn't feeling witty and flirtatious. He was feeling edgy, gritty, angry almost. He could pretend easily enough. He knew how to put on a mask and hide his emotions behind a wall of casual insouciance that nothing could ruffle, but Sambit already knew that side of him. If he wanted more than he'd had with past boyfriends, he had to offer more, and Sambit wouldn't take that first step, not when he still thought Derek's interest wouldn't last. Derek would have to take the first step and be the one to show Sambit his cards.

He booted up his laptop while he made a sandwich for lunch, then sat down to compose an e-mail. He could call, but it was still working hours for Sambit. More importantly, on the phone, Derek would be doubly exposed. Once for bringing down the wall around his emotions and twice for doing it without the filter of the written word. He wasn't sure he was quite ready for that yet. He'd have to get there eventually if he really wanted Sambit in his life, but it could wait another day or two.

Hi, Sam,

I hope you don't mind the e-mail instead of texts, but I had too much to say to break it into short little bursts. I'll text later to check on your head.

It's been rough being home. My generator is still working, fortunately, so I have power, but that's about all. The water from the tap smells so bad I almost don't want to take a shower (so I held my nose and thought of you last night). Floodwater must have gotten in the system at some point. The whole area reeks of it. I took Fido for a walk this morning and couldn't go more than about two steps without him stopping to smell something else.

It's bad here. Not just the contaminated water (and yes, I have bottled water to drink. I'm not going to get sick), but the downed trees and branches, telephone poles cracked in half, roads buckled... it's miserable. We found a couple of drowned animals as we were walking. They might have been dogs that got trapped by the rising flood and couldn't get to higher ground, but between the scavengers and just decomposition, it's impossible to tell now. I'm kind of ashamed to say it, but I lost my breakfast when we found the first one. We finished our walk and I spent more than a few minutes patting Fido when we got home. That could have been him out there. And yes, I know, I didn't know him before the storm so I wouldn't know to care if it had been him, but I care now, and that changes everything.

I haven't seen anyone else in the neighborhood since I got back. I know I'm a bit of a loner, but I do wave when I see my neighbors out working in their yards and stuff. I wonder where they all ended up. I wouldn't call any of them friends in the sense of hanging out with them on the weekends and stuff, but I wouldn't wish any of them ill. Well, other than the ones who abandoned Fido, but maybe there were extenuating circumstances, something that kept them from getting back home to take him with them. If they come back, I'll let them know that Fido's safe, but they can't have him back. I rescued him so he's mine now.

I need to start cleaning up in the yard, cutting up the fallen branches and raking the leaves, but I'm not going to do it now. It's hot and humid on top of everything else. I'd give myself heatstroke in about ten minutes trying to work outside now. I'll do a couple of hours after dinner and then do some more in the morning.

The good news, if you can call anything good at this point, is that I can't find any damage to the house other than a few missing shingles. I kept the extras from the original roof so I can patch the holes even if I end up having the roof redone. That'll probably depend on insurance, but I almost hate to apply for compensation when all I need is a new

*roof compared to some of the houses around me that'll have to be torn
down and rebuilt from the ground up. I haven't seen any sign of FEMA
or other officials yet other than the National Guard truck that rumbled
by this morning. The soldier who dropped me off yesterday said he'd
let them know I was here so they could check on me.*

*I don't know what their role is besides providing some security,
but maybe I should ask if there are ways I can help. I talked with
Kenneth, my boss, and he said it would be at least another week before
they expect people back at work so that gives me some time. I'm not
involved in any active missions at the moment, and I was actually
ahead of schedule on the next Mars explorer, so I'm not too worried
about missing a few days of work. If I can get enough gas for my
chainsaw, I can help clear downed trees. I can't restring power lines,
but I can help make it possible for the trucks to get through. I wonder
who I'd need to contact about helping. Any ideas?*

*Fido is whining at the door again, although I think that's because
he sees a squirrel in the backyard rather than because he needs to go
out. I guess it's a good sign that some of the wildlife survived. The ones
that could get above the floodwaters anyway and that weren't knocked
out of the trees by the wind.*

*Is it unmasculine of me to feel sad at the thought of the local
fauna suffering through the storm without even the barrier of a
building between them and the elements? I guess if it is, I'll just have to
live with it since I can't seem to stop shuddering every time I think of it.*

*Do me a favor the next time a hurricane comes this way. If I give
you that bullshit about it not coming our way or not being as bad as
they say or whatever stupid crap I said before this storm, knock me
over the head and drag me somewhere safe, okay? I look around me
and realize it's a miracle I survived. If I'd been in a different house, I
could be dead right now.*

Derek paused in his writing, his finger hovering over the delete
key as he reread the two last paragraphs. Of everything he had written,
they seemed the most revealing, and he felt the vulnerability of the
admission keenly. He didn't think Sambit would mock him for it, but
his instincts to self-protection ran deep. He had to take a couple of deep
breaths to override the need to retreat behind those walls again. Finally

the need to connect with Sambit in a truly meaningful way rather than through flirtatious quips won out, and he left the paragraphs in place.

How are the robots doing?

It was a copout, a retreat away from his vulnerability, but leaving the paragraphs there was the best he could do at the moment. Adding to them was beyond him.

I meant it when I said you should call me if you have problems with either of them. I can walk you through repairs or modifications to their programming, and if that still doesn't work, I can create a patch and e-mail the file to you so you can download it and install it that way. Things are bad enough where you are without malfunctioning technology making it worse.

Say hi to Lyrica for me, but please don't let her read this. Some of the things I said are for your eyes only. Of course, my luck, she was reading over your shoulder the whole time. Maybe I should put personal in the subject line so you know it's just for you rather than something about the robots that anyone could read.

He paused, trying to decide how to close the e-mail. "Sincerely" seemed too formal. "Yours" seemed too intimate. "Love" was out of the question at the moment. He settled finally for simply typing his name. Sambit could attribute whatever sentiment he wanted to the closing, and if he chose to attribute none at all, that was still better than an empty phrase.

He skimmed the e-mail once more, checking for typos or anything else embarrassing, but other than his e-mail program insisting unmasculine wasn't a word (he knew that, but it was the perfect word so he used it anyway), he didn't find anything to correct. Taking a deep breath and hoping he wasn't making a mistake, he hit Send.

"Okay, Fido, that's done," he said, looking across the room to the corner by the fireplace that Fido had claimed as his own. "What shall we do now?"

A knock on the door startled him. Fido raced toward the door, barking loudly. Derek hoped that would run off anyone with ill intent, but he clipped his pistol to his belt just in case. A check out through the window revealed a woman in a military uniform. He grabbed Fido's collar in case the dog decided to charge and cracked the door. "Yes?"

"Mr. Marshall?"

"Yes, I'm Derek Marshall." He didn't bother correcting the title she used. In this context his PhD was pretty much worthless.

"Pvt. Walters from Charlie Company told me you were here," she explained. "I'm Corporal Denise Murphy with the National Guard. I told him I'd come by and check on you."

"I'm doing okay," Derek said. "I stocked up with food and water before the storm hit, and I have plenty of fuel for the generator."

"Good," Cpl. Murphy said, handing him a card. "Here's my number if you need to reach me should there be a problem."

"Actually," Derek said, "I have a question for you. I'm sitting around here with nothing to do. Could y'all use another pair of hands? I've got a chainsaw. If nothing else, I can cut up some fallen trees, help get a few roads open."

"You'd have to agree to follow orders just like everyone else," Cpl. Murphy said. "We have pretty strict rules for putting civilians in jeopardy. No rushing into damaged buildings or anything like that, but every pair of hands helps where clearing roads are concerned."

"Let me just get my tools," Derek said, "and I can come with you now. Would it be all right if I brought my dog? He's friendly despite the barking."

"That's up to you," she said, "but you'll be responsible for him."

Derek looked down at Fido. "Maybe you better stay here, big guy. I don't know what kind of conditions we'll be working in, and I wouldn't want you to get lost or hurt. You can stay here and sleep, and I'll be home in a few hours to feed you dinner."

Fido whined and fretted as Derek gathered his belongings.

"I'm not going to abandon you," Derek promised, kneeling down to scratch Fido's muzzle and ears. "I'm going to work for a few hours, and then I'll be back. What are we going to do when I have to go back to NASA if you can't let me out of your sight, huh?"

"Did the storm traumatize him?" Cpl. Murphy asked sympathetically.

"His owners left him in a house that fell down around his ears," Derek explained, his voice hard. "I found him after it was over. He's bound to have abandonment issues after that."

"Bring him with you," Murphy said. "We can put him on a leash in the back of one of the trucks. That way he can see you but still be safe. No need to traumatize the poor thing even more."

"Thanks," Derek said, "although he'll have to get used to being alone eventually. My boss won't let me bring him to work."

"Nobody's going to be working anywhere around here anytime soon," Murphy said. "I haven't seen anything like this outside of pictures of bombing sites."

"I work at NASA," Derek said. "From what my boss said, they'll be ready to let people back in to work within a week."

"But that assumes people can get there," Murphy said. "I haven't been down that way specifically, but I don't know that you could get there from here at the moment."

"Well, let's see what we can do about fixing that."

BY THE time Sambit finished his shift that day, he was ready to throw things. Tucker had been absolutely intolerable all day, making unreasonable demands of both the people and the machines at the plant to the point that Sambit was tempted to tell him to shove it and leave. The only problem was transportation. He had no way of getting home.

Rubbing at his temples to fight the pounding headache, he collapsed on his cot and stared at the ceiling, wishing Derek were there. He hadn't gotten any texts today, not that he'd really expected to. Hoped to, yes, but not expected. Not really. He lay there for a few minutes, fighting exhaustion and apathy, before forcing himself to sit up and open his e-mail. If nothing else, he should send his parents a note to let them know how he was doing. He'd sent them a short message after the hurricane passed letting them know he was safe, but that was over a week ago. They'd start worrying if he didn't send something again soon.

At the top of his inbox was a message from Derek.

Sambit smiled, his headache receding slightly. He clicked on the message and began to read. The first few lines made him smile as he thought of the text messages he and Derek had exchanged the day before. He might deny he was flirting when Lyrica asked, but in the privacy of his own thoughts, he knew he'd been doing just that. Derek made it so easy.

He sobered somewhat as he read the next few paragraphs.

I'm kind of ashamed to say it, but I lost my breakfast when we found the first one.

The admission surprised Sambit. He wasn't surprised Derek had gotten sick at the sight of the dead and decaying animal, but he was surprised Derek had admitted it. Not many men would. They'd act strong and stoic, saying it was a shame the animals died, perhaps, but not owning up to the kind of reaction that would lead to throwing up all over the sidewalk. Derek went up a couple of notches in Sambit's esteem for his honesty.

Derek's protectiveness toward Fido didn't surprise Sambit at all. He'd seen enough of it when Derek and Fido had been at the power plant with him. If the dog's original owners thought they were getting anywhere near him, they had another think coming, even if they did have an explanation for what had happened. Derek might have rescued the animal out of a sense of duty or a kind heart, but Fido was his now, there was no doubt about that.

The part about working outside but waiting until it was cooler made Sambit smile. He could imagine Derek outside working in his yard, his T-shirt tucked into the back of his shorts as he tried to catch every hint of breeze from the Gulf. The thought was not designed to help his composure, so Sambit forced his attention back to the e-mail in front of him.

His heart skipped a couple of beats as he read on and came to Derek's comment about the local wildlife. It was that same protective nature but put on center stage, spotlighted, underlined, and with a red arrow pointing at it in case Sambit had missed it, and beneath that protective nature, a heart tender enough to be disturbed by the death of the creatures around him. *You could never be unmasculine.* He'd typed the words into the reply even before he finished reading the rest of the e-mail, but that much had to be said no matter what else he typed or didn't type in reply.

If I give you that bullshit about it not coming our way or not being as bad as they say or whatever stupid crap I said before this storm, knock me over the head and drag me somewhere safe, okay? I look around me and realize it's a miracle I survived. If I'd been in a different house, I could be dead right now.

And I'll hold you to that bit about leaving the next time there's a storm, Sambit added as he read the next paragraph. He had rolled his eyes and shaken his head when Derek had told him he'd ridden out the storm at home, but now, seeing Derek's descriptions of the destruction, it drove home to Sambit how close he'd come to losing Derek before he ever met him. *You don't get to scare me like that again, understood?*

The sudden change of subject after that was as telling as the content of the two previous paragraphs. Derek had gotten uncomfortable being that open and retreated to something safe. Sambit didn't even mind. Derek had shared a side of himself Sambit suspected few people ever got to see. Sambit could live with seeing that side again. He'd have to find ways to encourage that.

Lyrica has gone to sleep, I think, but I'll say hi to her from you in the morning. Even if she isn't asleep, I'm ready for some downtime.

Tucker was even more impossible than usual today. He's got it in his head that we can use the robots to drain the radioactive water from the turbines, get in the heat exchanger and fix the leaking pipes, and somehow get this reactor back online again. I suppose it's possible in theory to fix the heat exchanger, but not without a lot more time and equipment than we have here. And not without a lot more danger to the people doing the work. No offense to your robots, but I don't know if this is something that can be done remotely. The sheer magnitude of the work involved is mind-boggling to me. I keep hoping saner heads will prevail, but no one here at the moment has the authority to supersede Tucker so we're stuck trying to protect ourselves and not get fired at the same time.

Before you ask, my dosimeter is .28 today, and yes, I have a headache, but I'm pretty sure his name is Tucker rather than radiation sickness.

I don't know what to do. It's so ingrained in me to follow instructions and obey authority when I'm given an order, but I know Tucker's orders are foolhardy at best. At worst, they could be fatal. Maybe not to me since I probably won't be around long enough to see the kind of work he's proposing get started, but I'd hate to see Lyrica or anyone else exposed to that level of danger.

I shouldn't dump all this on you. There's really nothing you can do about it. I just needed to tell someone. If everything goes horribly wrong, there will be a record of my concerns and the fact that I voiced them to Tucker and was ignored.

Sambit hit send before he could reconsider the wisdom of sharing his concerns with Derek.

He closed his eyes and lay back on his cot. His head ached, but rubbing his temples with his own fingers didn't work nearly as well as Derek's massage had done. He wished he had a better plan than just letting Derek know about his concerns, but he didn't really know who else to contact. Lyrica might, but she'd been surprisingly silent all day, letting Sambit bear the brunt of Tucker's idiocy. He could possibly send an e-mail to his department chair at Texas A&M. He might know someone higher up at the NRC who could override Tucker's orders. He'd send an e-mail tomorrow.

The sound of his phone ringing jarred him out of his doze. He picked it up, hoping it was someone he could ignore so he could go to sleep. Derek's name flashed across the screen. He smiled. That was even better.

"Hi, Derek."

"If Tucker orders you to do something dangerous, you refuse. If you can use the robot to do it, fine, but if it means exposing yourself to excess radiation, you refuse."

"He hasn't asked us to do anything dangerous yet," Sambit assured Derek, the fire in the other man's voice reassuring him that someone would be on his side if it came down to a fight with Tucker.

"If he does, call me," Derek said. "Then put on a radiation suit and start walking. It'll take me an hour or two to get there on my bike depending on what shape the roads are in, but I'll leave the minute you call. You aren't a plant employee, and you aren't in the military. Tucker can't make you put yourself in harm's way."

"It'll take more than two hours to ride a bike here," Sambit said, although he was certain Derek meant a motorcycle. "I appreciate the offer, though."

"It's a motorcycle and you know it," Derek snapped, "and if I find out you didn't take me up on it and did something dangerous instead, I'll come up there and get you myself."

"I won't do anything dangerous without believing it's the right thing to do," Sambit promised. He wasn't going to promise not to do anything dangerous at all. He knew better than to think he could keep *that* promise.

"Not good enough," Derek said through the phone, his voice a deep growl.

It warmed Sambit's heart to know Derek was so invested in his safety. "It's the best you're going to get. I don't want to think about Tucker anymore. Tell me about the rest of your day instead. Did you get your yard cleaned up?"

"No, the National Guard knocked on my door to check on me, and I ended up volunteering with them for the rest of the day," Derek said. "I'm exhausted and wishing I trusted the water enough to take a hot bath, but we got a big section of Broadway cleared from 288 down to Cullen. It was slow going with all the trees and debris from the flooding, but there's a power station in that stretch, so the utility company can come in and start repairs working out from there as soon as they have the personnel in place. I asked around, but nobody had any real idea how long that would take. I guess they don't have a lot of experience with this degree of disaster."

"I don't imagine they do," Sambit said. "The only thing in recent memory that even comes close is Katrina, and while that was awful, the biggest problem there was the levees breaking and the flooding. This was an entirely different caliber of storm. The water may have gone down faster, but the wind damage has to be worse."

"We certainly had scads of trees down along Broadway," Derek agreed. "Some of the sections along there aren't developed, just big expanses of trees. We didn't even try to get back in there to see what shape they were in. We just cleared the ones from the road. Nature will have to take care of the rest. Or some developer when the area starts coming back."

"So are you feeling better or worse about the state of things now that you've spent the day helping out?" Sambit asked, the despair implicit in Derek's e-mail still fresh in his mind.

"It's hard to feel better when you see how bad it really is," Derek replied, "but at the same time, it helped to do something, you know? To not feel like I was sitting around on my ass all day doing nothing when there were people out there working hard. They wouldn't let me go in any of the buildings or help with any of the search and rescue stuff the local police and fire people were doing. They said I was a civilian, and they weren't authorized to put me at risk. So, see? I'm being good. You have to do the same. Why did your dosimeter reading go up three rads today? Did you go outside?"

"For a few minutes," Sambit admitted. "I had to get away from Tucker. Lyrica's defense was to simply not say anything, which left me to try to make him see reason. I should have followed her example, but I was afraid if I did, he'd order us to do something stupid, so I argued with him. I reached the point where it was go outside or punch him. I thought going outside was the preferable option."

"Punch him next time," Derek said, "or else put on a hazmat suit before you go outside. That's too much of a jump for one day. I don't want you getting sick."

"Or what? You'll come get me?" Sambit teased.

"If I have to. I appreciate your determination to help while they're shorthanded, but this is not your job," Derek said. "You don't have to endanger your health doing this."

".28 Gray isn't enough to hurt me," Sambit assured him. "If I were exposed to that level of radiation constantly over the course of months or years, it might, but not for the few weeks I'll be here. I know you don't believe me, but I'm not trying to get sick. I just needed to breathe air that hadn't been recycled who knows how many times for a few minutes. I needed to feel the wind on my face, even if it's a hundred degrees, and see the blue sky and listen to the birds chirping. They're coming back too."

"Mother Nature is a lot better at recovering from disasters than we are," Derek said, "but that's changing the subject. Please take care of yourself. I want to see you again when this is over, and not in the hospital."

"Aw, you won't come sit at my bedside if I get sick?"

"Don't even joke about it," Derek snapped. "Not about that. It's too easy to die from radiation sickness. I'd never forgive myself for leaving without you if that happened."

There it was, that protective nature over a tender heart again. It never failed to tug at Sambit. He didn't know how he'd ended up on the receiving end of that protectiveness, but he couldn't make himself complain about it. Not when it made Derek so attractive.

"I'll be careful," Sambit promised. "I don't want to end up in the hospital either."

"Is your head still bothering you?"

"Not nearly as much now," Sambit said. "I think just talking to you helped. Maybe I'll get a good night's sleep, and Tucker won't seem nearly so annoying in the morning."

"Sleep well," Derek said. "I'd tuck you in and give you a good night kiss if I were there, but you'll have to settle for a long distance one since I'm not."

Sambit chuckled. "I'm sure I'll manage to sleep without being tucked in. Thanks for listening, Derek. Really."

"Anytime," Derek replied. "Send me a text in the morning and let me know if you're feeling better."

"You don't have to babysit me. I can take care of myself."

"I know you can, but indulge me. What can it hurt?"

"Fine," Sambit said. "I'll text you in the morning."

"I tried doing yoga when I got home tonight, thinking it would help relax my muscles."

Sambit smiled, thrilled at the thought that Derek had continued the practice even after he left. "And?"

"And I landed on my ass within the first five minutes. I miss your guiding hand on my... shoulder." The pause lasted so long Sambit knew Derek had changed his mind about what he was going to say. It surprised him, actually, that Derek would rein in his flirting that much.

"Keep practicing. It'll get easier, I promise."

"I just need you to keep teaching me," Derek insisted.

"We'll see," Sambit said. "I should really go to sleep now."

"Text me in the morning," Derek repeated.

"I will. Good night."

"Good night, Sambit."

Derek ended the call before Sambit could reply or comment on his use of Sambit's full name, but the effect was undeniable. His name in Derek's voice needed to be on a list of controlled substances, because Sambit's body had tensed at the sound in anticipation of being touched like Derek had done in the shower before he left. Unfortunately that wasn't going to happen tonight with Derek back in Houston and Sambit still in Bay City. He'd just have to think of other things until he fell asleep.

chapter
FOURTEEN

WHEN Sambit's phone rang a week later, he smiled as he picked it up, already knowing who would be on the other end. He and Derek had e-mailed or texted every day since Derek's departure and had talked on the phone for at least a few minutes almost every night. There had been one night when Sambit was so tired and his head hurt so badly that he'd sent Derek an e-mail saying he was going to bed and to please not call until tomorrow. Derek's reply e-mail had been concerned, making Sambit promise to call him in the morning instead, but he'd respected Sambit's wishes. The phone call the next morning had been full of repeated offers to come get him, followed quickly by Lyrica saying Derek wanted to know what his dosimeter reading was. It hadn't gone up in two days so Sambit didn't mind her telling Derek, and Derek's concern had put a smile on Sambit's face for most of the morning.

"Hi, Derek."

"How's your head tonight?

"It's okay," Sambit said. "I'm tired, but no headache."

"Really?" Derek's voice betrayed his skepticism.

"Really. Tucker got called into some meeting today and wasn't at the plant so he wasn't adding to the stress of the situation. When he got back, he said we should be getting more staff and maybe some portable trailers and better beds and stuff. It'll be another week, maybe two, but the NRC is working with FEMA to set something up."

"That's good news! Everyone will be more comfortable that way. So will they let you leave once the new staff arrives?"

"Not right away, probably," Sambit said. "I'm still the best robot operator they have, thanks to you, not to mention the only one at the moment who has any idea how to do any repairs on it. Unless the new staff includes another robotics engineer, I'm probably stuck until classes start again."

"I'd be happier if you were back in College Station."

"So would I," Sambit said, "but Tucker hasn't decided to get rid of me yet, and I don't have a compelling reason to leave so it feels a little like abandoning my post. Enough about me. Tell me about your day."

"Same old," Derek replied. "Worked with FEMA and the National Guard again, but we got some good news too. They certified the water as safe again so I'm taking a bath."

"That will be relaxing," Sambit said, more than a little envious. "I won't keep you long so you can go enjoy it."

"No," Derek said, his voice full of sly humor and something warmer and more seductive, "I'm taking a bath now. I'm sitting here in a tub full of hot water, thinking about you and wishing you were here with me."

Heat shot through Sambit at the image of Derek in the tub, long body stretched out along cool marble, steam rising from the water and wreathing his face. "We are *not* having phone sex."

"Awww, why not?"

"Because I'm sitting in Lyrica's office, and even though I have the door locked, you never know when someone will come knocking, and this is where I work, which makes it totally inappropriate." He was babbling, but he couldn't seem to stop. If he did, Derek would start talking again, and Sambit already knew he wouldn't listen to admonitions.

"Convenient excuses. That's fine. We don't have to have phone sex. I'll just lie here and talk to you and jerk off to the sound of your voice."

That did nothing to help restore Sambit's equilibrium. "You shouldn't."

"Why not? I love the sound of your voice. You have the hint of an accent that makes your voice incredibly sexy. It's probably a good thing I'm not in one of your classes. I'd never learn anything because I'd be too distracted and turned on by your voice to make sense of what you were saying."

Sambit felt his skin flush hot. He had managed to adopt a fairly American vocabulary after all the time he'd lived here, but he still hadn't lost the hint of India in his voice, an almost singsongish rhythm that always made him self-conscious when he was speaking in public. Not in class—that wasn't public—but at forums or other events. Now he'd be even more on edge every time, remembering Derek's comment about his voice.

"Don't say things like that," he said, his voice hoarse as he reacted to Derek's seduction. He wouldn't give Derek the satisfaction of joining him in jerking off, but he was helpless to control his body's reaction to the tantalizing image of Derek on the other end of the phone.

"Okay." Derek's voice was deep and soft, lulling Sambit into complacency. "I'll close my eyes and remember what it felt like to touch you. Do you have any idea how good you felt under my hands? Your skin was so hot, smooth with just the right dusting of hair to remind me I had my hands on a real man, not some twinky kid with too much testosterone and not enough sense. And the way you moved with me…. I'm hard just thinking about it. Fuck, Sambit. I'm not going to last long at this rate. Are you sure you wouldn't rather talk to me instead? It would slow things down, because if I touch myself thinking about what it felt like to push against you, I'm going to come in no time."

Sambit couldn't answer, the memory of showering with Derek too fresh and too powerful for him to summon words. He swore he could feel Derek's callused hands moving over his skin again, and the sound of his name in that deep husky voice was too seductive to ignore.

"No?" Derek said. "That's fine. I'll talk to you, then. I wish you were here. I'd pull you in the tub with me, right onto my lap, between my legs, back to front so I could touch you like I did before, your body all open and spread out for me to enjoy. You'd enjoy it too. I'd work your dick just the way you like, slow and then fast and then slow again, drawing it out as long as possible, until you were begging for me to stop, to hurry, to let you come, to fuck you, anything."

Sambit groaned. He could imagine it so easily. He'd do it, too, if they were together. He wasn't one to make a lot of noise during sex, but Derek could drive him to it with his teasing and his control, because Sambit already knew Derek would never be a selfish lover. He might take his own pleasure once he'd seen to Sambit's, but it would never be at the expense of Sambit's needs.

"You'd be so tight when I pushed you up onto your knees," Derek went on. "I know you. You don't sleep around. It's probably been months since someone last fucked you."

"Two years," Sambit admitted hoarsely.

"Shit, you'd be as tight as a virgin again after that long," Derek said, his voice breaking. "I'd be careful popping your cherry all over again. I'd make it so good for you. I swear I would."

"I know," Sambit whispered.

"Let me do it," Derek pleaded. "Let me inside you."

Sambit didn't answer. He couldn't. His whole body clenched at the thought of being on his knees with Derek behind him, preparing him, penetrating him, fucking him into oblivion. It wouldn't take much, not as turned on as he was at the moment.

Derek took his silence as a refusal. "If you won't let me do that, I'll find some other way to make you feel good. I give a damn good blow job. I'd dry you off and spread you out on the bed and lick every inch of your body. Every inch, Sambit, until you couldn't stand it a second longer, and then I'd find your dick. I'd have to lick the puddle off your stomach first or I'd have a mess all over my face. When that was clean, I'd work on the rest of you, licking and sucking until you were desperate to fuck my face, but I'd hold your hips down so you had to lie there and take it."

Sambit groaned. He could all but feel Derek's mouth on him. The urge to touch himself was nearly irresistible, but he didn't reach for his cock. He didn't trust what might come out of his mouth if he started participating in this. He'd end up begging Derek to come get him, and

Derek would do it, but that didn't make it a good idea. Nothing could make it a good idea.

"I'd draw it out as long as I could," Derek went on, his breath coming in harsh pants over the phone. Sambit could tell he was close. A word or two would push Derek over the edge, but Sambit remained silent, holding on to the tenuous connection. "But eventually you wouldn't be able to stand it any longer, your balls drawn up tight, your whole body trembling with the need to come. I'd swallow you all the way down and you'd lose it right there in my throat, giving me everything you've got. I'd keep sucking and swallowing until you were so sensitive you had to pull away because that's what makes it good, drawing it out until you just can't take any more."

Sambit already couldn't take it anymore just from the images Derek was putting in his head. The reality would probably kill him. "And then?" Sambit whispered. "What about you?"

"You'd take care of me," Derek said. "It wouldn't take much. A hand on my prick or maybe a kiss. Give me a kiss, Sambit, and it'll be all over."

Sambit felt ridiculous making kissing noises over the phone, but Derek's hoarse moan made it clear Derek didn't find the situation ridiculous at all. Desire hit Sambit hard as he imagined what Derek must look like, his cock in his hand, sticky from his release, lying replete in the tub. The only thing missing was Sambit in the tub with him.

"I should go," Sambit said. "I'll e-mail you tomorrow."

He hung up before Derek could reply, his body aching with the need for release. His heart pounded so hard in his chest he could hardly catch his breath, the mixture of need and panic more than he could control. Grabbing his towel, he fled to the restroom where Derek had installed the shower. He barely had the forethought to hang the shower sign outside before locking the door. He stripped as fast as he could, tearing a button off his shirt in his haste. The water hit him in a hot stream, and he swore he could feel Derek's hands on him, Derek's body behind him.

He wanted to take his time, but he couldn't wait. A few pulls later, he spilled all over his hand, Derek's name on his lips.

He lingered after that, taking the time to shower and regain his composure. He didn't know if he'd meet anyone in the halls going back to Lyrica's office, but he didn't want to take the risk of being flustered if he did.

When he finally felt in control again, he dried off and headed back to the office. His phone blinked at him when he moved it to the side. He swiped his finger across it, bringing up a text from Derek.

Did you jerk off in the shower?

No, of course not. The denial was automatic, not that he'd have told Derek anyway. Some things were private.

Then what took you so long to reply? You did jerk off. Come on, you can admit it to me. I just gave myself a hand job with you listening in. You can't possibly be embarrassed to tell me.

It probably was a silly reaction given what he'd shared with Derek, but Sambit was embarrassed. He didn't lose control like that. Ever. Except that he'd done it with alarming frequency since he met Derek.

Fine. I jerked off in the shower. Are you happy now?

I won't be happy until you're here with me.

How the hell was he supposed to respond to that? Sambit wondered. Derek had just changed it from sex to something else. Sambit didn't put a name on it. He couldn't think of it as a relationship, not if he wanted to keep a modicum of distance to protect himself when Derek grew bored with traveling back and forth between College Station and Pearland. He was already surprised by Derek's continued interest, but he wasn't back at work yet, back to his normal routine. He hadn't mentioned any of his neighbors returning after the storm or any contact from anyone at work other than his boss, that first day, so things were hardly typical. All the things that would normally occupy Derek's time were still absent, leaving him with nothing to do but chat with Sambit. Once he had those things back, he'd lose interest.

I didn't scare you off, did I?

Of course not. There just didn't seem to be anything else to say.

Oh. Well, sleep well then.

"Damn it," Sambit muttered. He'd managed to hurt Derek's feelings. He couldn't have said how he knew when all he had were the words in a text message, but he knew. If Derek had been there, his voice would have been clipped and tight, his face a mask of indifference, but Sambit had seen behind that mask to the tender heart that hid beneath it. He'd just nicked that heart when the last thing he wanted to do was hurt either of them.

I'm sorry. I didn't mean to upset you. I just don't know how to answer comments like that.

Say you'll let me come visit you after you leave. If I'm wrong and everything is all awkward, I won't visit again, but let me see you once more no matter what.

All right.

He knew it was a mistake. He'd end up alone again, just like he had when Praveen got married while Sambit was working on his PhD. Derek, at least, would have the good grace to tell Sambit if he decided to move on. He wouldn't have to hear the news from his mother, a scant month after he left Hyderabad for the States.

He shouldn't still be bitter about it all these years later, but the passage of time hadn't lessened his sense of betrayal. He knew what Praveen would say. He'd talk about family pressure and the realities of life in India and Sambit being away, and Sambit even knew some of that was true. His family had put plenty of pressure on him to let them arrange a marriage for him, but unlike Praveen, he'd refused. The fear lingered, though. If he couldn't hold the attention of Praveen, with whom he'd had everything in common except his commitment to their relationship, how could he hold Derek's attention when they had nothing in common except a few tense days during a nuclear disaster?

Unfortunately he'd passed the point of cutting ties on his end. He wanted Derek's attention, however fleeting it ended up being. He wouldn't hold Derek to his promise to visit, of course, but that was a problem for later. For now, he had to get some sleep. He turned off his phone so it wouldn't vibrate if Derek texted back and tried to get comfortable on the cot. No matter which way he turned, though, it felt like something was poking him in the back or the side. He got up and tried to do some yoga, but that didn't help either.

Pulling on the least disgusting of his clothes—he hoped FEMA would make provisions for laundry as well as sleeping quarters—he left the office to pace the halls. He ran into Lyrica coming back from the shower.

"I figured you'd be asleep already," she said with a smile for him. "Or else on the phone with Derek."

"I talked to Derek already tonight," Sambit said, grateful his dark complexion hid the heat he could feel staining his cheeks. "I tried sleeping, but I couldn't get comfortable. I was thinking about going for a walk."

"Not the healthiest thing to do around here," Lyrica reminded him. "Why don't you come sit with me and tell me what's on your mind? It has to be something because you don't usually have problems falling asleep."

Sambit was afraid that was a bad, bad idea, but he followed her anyway because no matter how bad an idea baring his soul to Lyrica was, it was still healthier than going outside at the moment.

They went into the smaller office Lyrica had commandeered for her bedroom. She gestured for him to take the desk chair while she sat on the cot, shifting around a bit until she could find a comfortable position. "That's part of my problem," Sambit said. "No matter how I lie down, I can't get comfortable."

"But that's been an issue the whole time we've been here so that isn't what's keeping you awake tonight. Did you have a fight with Derek?"

"I didn't think we had, but I'm afraid he thinks we did," Sambit admitted. "He... he's interested in me."

"Tell me something I don't know," Lyrica retorted. "A blind man could have seen that when he was still here. And you're interested in him, so what's the problem?"

"I'm here and he's not," Sambit said. "That never works."

"Okay, maybe I'd agree with you if you said he was in India and you were here," Lyrica said, the echo of his past causing Sambit to flinch. "Oh, I struck a nerve there, didn't I?"

Sambit nodded. "This isn't the first time I've tried a long-distance relationship. They're a recipe for disaster."

"I don't know the whole story, obviously, unless you'd care to share, but I think you're underestimating Derek and overestimating the problem," Lyrica said. "My comparison aside, you aren't talking about an insurmountable distance with Derek, or only being able to see each other once or twice a year. Once we get out of here, you could easily see him every weekend, even if you didn't see him during the week."

"That might work for a while, but I don't want to 'date' him forever. If I'm going to be with someone, I want a life together, and two hours apart doesn't constitute that."

"Now you're jumping ahead and borrowing trouble," Lyrica scolded. "For all you know, Derek could do a lot of his work from home, and if that's the case, then it doesn't matter where he lives. You could look into doing more online classes and seminars. I know a lot of universities are going to that model now so they can offer classes in certain areas even if they don't have the faculty on site. I have a cousin in Austin who teaches photography classes remotely for a university in San Francisco. So maybe you don't have to be on campus every day. Even if that doesn't work, you could split the difference. People in Houston regularly drive an hour or more for their commute without thinking anything of it. It's not what you're used to, but that doesn't mean you couldn't do it. You'd even be going against rush hour traffic driving to A&M in the morning."

"So you're saying I should stop worrying and give it a try."

"I'm asking what you have to lose," Lyrica said. "Okay, if it doesn't work out, your heart might be a little battered, but you have this fabulous man interested in you, and from what I could tell while he was here, if he's interested in you, he'll treat you like a king. You could be passing up a chance at something really, really good because some idiot in India wasn't smart enough to see what a wonderful man he had in you. That doesn't make you a bad catch. It makes him stupid. Derek is a lot of things, and maybe if some of those are issues, you should think about it again, but one thing he isn't is stupid."

Sambit considered everything he knew about Derek, all their interactions, positive and negative. He might not like Derek's cursing, but Derek was trying to curb it. Derek might not understand Sambit's desire to keep certain things private, but he hadn't told anyone else Sambit was gay. Derek hadn't belittled him for his yoga or done any of the other things some of Sambit's past lovers had done to make him doubt himself, and the sex....

Sambit couldn't remember the last time he'd had someone pay as much attention to his needs as Derek had done in the shower. He'd been completely gutted by his orgasm, and the one in the shower a few minutes ago, after talking to Derek on the phone, had been almost as powerful. He knew they'd fight sometimes, but he didn't think it would be over anything important. In a bubble, he and Derek could work quite well as a couple. If only they didn't have to deal with all the outside stuff.

"What are you brooding about?" Lyrica demanded.

"All the reasons any relationship is a bad idea for me," Sambit admitted. "I'm not out at work or at temple or anywhere really. I don't need to be when I'm single. The aunties all shake their heads and cluck their tongues over the fact that I still haven't found some nice girl to take care of me, but they leave me alone after that. My colleagues don't blink when I show up at department functions alone because I've never brought anyone with me to events. I've never had anyone I cared to bring. It keeps things simple."

"Really, Sambit?" Lyrica said. "That's the best you can do? This isn't the Stone Age. Your colleagues won't care. The aunties might blink a few times, but if they say something, you tell them it's none of their business, or you find a different temple where they will accept you. Hell, Derek will probably charm them all right out of their disapproval if you let him."

He probably would at that. "I can't do anything about it from here anyway," Sambit said. "We'll see what happens when I leave. If Derek is still interested, maybe I'll see where it goes, but for now, it's better not to make promises he might not want me to keep."

"Just don't push him away in the meantime. You don't want to end up spending your life alone."

"Where's your partner?" Sambit countered.

"Believe me," Lyrica said. "If I've learned something from being here, it's that I don't want to have no one to miss me if I didn't come home. I'll be doing some reevaluating as soon as I'm safely out of here."

"And you think I should do the same."

"Yes, I do."

chapter
FIFTEEN

"I HEARD from my boss today. He said they have clearance for people to come back to work as soon as they can," Derek said.

Sambit nodded, the webcam allowing Derek to see his gestures as well as hear his voice. "So when will you go back?"

"Tomorrow," Derek said. "There's no reason to wait. I can get there safely. I checked that out a couple of days ago. I've been helping with the National Guard because every pair of hands helps, but I'm not critical personnel. They won't miss me if I go back to work, and my project does have a deadline, even if it's still a while off."

"You don't have to justify your decision to me," Sambit reminded him. "I was curious, nothing more." He was nervous, but he wasn't going to tell Derek that. Tomorrow would mean the end of their steady stream of texts during the day and the e-mail from Derek waiting for him when he got off his shift tomorrow evening. It would mean a return to Derek's normal routine and the beginning of the end of his interest in Sambit, but he didn't say any of that. Derek would deny it, and Sambit couldn't bear to hear promises he knew couldn't be kept.

"What about you?" Derek asked. "Any word on the FEMA trailers?"

"They're supposed to get here tomorrow, the next day at the latest," Sambit said. "I'm ready. I swear this cot gets more uncomfortable every night. I don't know how soldiers in the field do it."

"The same way you are," Derek replied. "They bitch and moan about it and keep going because that's what they do. I'm hearing the same complaints from the National Guard that I am from you about the cots, the weather, the gear they have to carry, and everything else."

"Well, one thing's for sure. I'll never complain about a lumpy mattress again. After three weeks on this cot, any mattress would be welcome."

"You can share mine anytime," Derek offered with a cheeky grin. Sambit couldn't help returning the smile. If Derek kept his promise and came to see Sambit after Sambit went home, that would be almost inevitable given the tension simmering beneath the surface every time they talked or texted. The e-mails were different, though. Not that Derek didn't sometimes flirt in those too, because he did, quite a bit at times, but he also shared sides of himself Sambit rarely saw anywhere else. Sambit had seen more kindness, more vulnerability, in Derek's e-mails than he would have believed possible given the façade Derek had adopted when they'd first met. He held on to those hints with both hands because they gave him the courage to keep answering the texts and to keep looking past the casual, or not so casual, flirting when they talked. Derek had trusted him enough to show hints of the man beneath the mask. Sambit nurtured a faint hope that the mask would someday fall completely.

Sambit half expected Derek to push Sambit for an answer, to turn the conversation into cybersex, but Derek let it go after that one brief comment, making Sambit fear he was already losing interest. Instead he talked about work, about the project he'd be going back to and the exploration his robot would eventually get to do on Mars and how maybe Venus was next and wouldn't it be amazing if they could eventually get a manned spacecraft to either planet.

It was an interesting discussion, the kind Sambit had often relished with his colleagues at Texas A&M, but it wasn't the kind of conversation he was used to having with Derek. He might not have minded if he hadn't needed the reassurance of Derek's continued interest, but tonight it only highlighted Sambit's fears. By the time they said good night, Sambit had given up hope of keeping Derek's interest for much longer.

THE next day passed pretty much as Sambit had predicted. He got a short text from Derek a little after noon saying he was on his lunch break, but by the time Sambit got a break himself to be able to answer, Derek had gone back to work and didn't reply until much later, by which point Sambit was busy again. The resulting lack of real contact left Sambit more than a little grumpy by the end of his shift.

"Did you and Derek have a fight?" Lyrica asked as they heated up dinner.

"No, he just went back to work today," Sambit explained.

"You should be excited for him," Lyrica said. "It had to be grating on him not to be busy."

"He was busy. He was helping with the recovery efforts," Sambit said, "but he sounded happy to be going back to work when we talked last night."

"Of course he's happy to be back at work," Lyrica said. "Won't you be happy to go back to teaching after this?"

"Actually I was thinking teaching might be kind of boring after all the hands-on work I've done here with you," Sambit said. "I wonder if it might be time to look for a job in industry instead of education. Not this semester certainly, and maybe not even until next summer, but I could start looking anyway."

"I'll gladly write a recommendation for you," Lyrica offered. "Tucker won't, but he's an idiot anyway. I talked to the plant owners today, and they're going to appeal to the NRC for a different representative. Maybe we'll get someone reasonable this time."

"Thank you," Sambit said, summoning a smile. She didn't deserve to bear the brunt of his bad mood. "I'll keep that in mind if I decide to go through with it."

"So what time are you going to call Derek?"

"I wasn't planning on calling him," Sambit said.

"Sambit, he just went back to work. You have to call and ask him how it went. You don't want him to think you're a bad boyfriend," Lyrica scolded.

"I'm not his boyfriend."

"Oh, really?" Lyrica said. "You haven't spent the past two weeks texting and e-mailing him on a regular basis, talking to him almost every night on the phone, and who knows what else? I'd say that constitutes boyfriends. Or have you forgotten about whatever happened in the shower?"

"I haven't forgotten anything," Sambit said, feeling his face heat at the memory of Derek's hands on him and of jerking off in the shower after they'd had phone sex. "That doesn't make us boyfriends."

"So what would?" Lyrica asked. "Seriously, what would make you a couple?"

Sambit hesitated, realizing he didn't actually have an answer to her question. "Um…."

"Maybe you should think about that," she said, "instead of telling yourself he'll never be interested in you. Figure out what you'd want a relationship with him to look like. Obviously there are limits because you're still stuck here, but this won't go on forever. What would you want when you leave?"

"I'll think about it," Sambit promised, taking his food from the microwave. "I'm going to eat in my room. I need some quiet for a bit."

"Eat wherever you want," Lyrica replied, "but call Derek."

"All right," Sambit said. "I will, but don't get your hopes up for the results."

Lyrica shook her head at him, but she didn't say anything else.

Sambit carried his plate of microwaved lasagna down to the office he used as a bedroom and sat down on the cot to eat. Or, more honestly, to push his food around the tray while he pondered Lyrica's insistence that he and Derek were already a couple despite Sambit's doubts.

They weren't in the same place at the moment, but other than that, when he thought about his parents and their relationship or the relationships of any of his friends, he couldn't think of a single thing other than sharing a bed at night that they did that he and Derek weren't already doing, and Sambit suspected that if Derek were still here, they'd even be doing that. The only thing missing was a stated commitment to the relationship, and that was only missing on Sambit's part. Derek had said multiple times that he wanted to see Sambit again, that he wanted to find a way to make things work between them even with the distance and everything else. It was more a matter of logistics than commitment according to Derek.

So now Sambit had to find a way to believe Derck's words.

Before he could follow that train of thought any further, his phone rang.

"Hello?"

"Hi, Sam. How was your day?"

"Hi, Derek. I didn't expect to hear from you so soon."

"I'm sorry I kept missing you today. It was a little crazy getting back to work after being off for so long."

"It's fine," Sambit said. "I didn't expect to hear from you even the little bit I did."

"Then I'm glad I could surprise you," Derek replied. "You didn't answer my question. How was your day?"

"Tucker was his usual stupid self, but Lyrica said the plant bosses were going to call the NRC, so that's good news," Sambit said. "And we got confirmation that the FEMA trailers will arrive tomorrow along with some additional staff."

"Wonderful!" Derek said. "You'll have a little more comfort and a little more privacy once that happens. And maybe even shorter shifts."

"I'll be glad not to work twelve-hour shifts anymore," Sambit agreed. "It's okay for a few days, but I'm worn out."

"You should be," Derek agreed. "But things should get easier tomorrow. Are the robots still holding up okay?"

"Mostly," Sambit said. "One of them has started having problems with one of its rollers. I sprayed it down with WD-40 like you said I might have to do, and that seems to have helped. I don't really want to have to take it apart and put it back together again. I'm not sure I'm that good."

"Yeah, those robots weren't designed for industrial use," Derek said. "I tweaked them as much as I could with the parts I had, but the grit from being outside and climbing over rocks will gum up the gears. Maybe they'll have someone in the new staff who has some experience with robots. If not, this weekend when I'm not working, we'll get on the webcam and I'll talk you through taking it apart to clean it out."

"That would be great," Sambit said. It wasn't what he wanted. He wanted Derek there to help him with it, or even better, to do it himself so Sambit didn't have to worry about screwing it up, but it was better than nothing. Remembering Lyrica's admonitions, he changed the subject. "How was *your* day? Glad to be back at work?"

"It was a mess," Derek said. "Despite all the precautions, parts of the building flooded and are still closed off because they're worried about mold. Half of my tools are in the quarantined section of the building. They're bringing things out slowly, but everything has to be sanitized and certified as safe to use again, which takes for-fucking-ever. Sorry about the language, but there's really no other way to describe it. So there I was trying to do my job and get back up to speed on my project with only half the things I would usually have at my disposal. I told Kenneth I was taking a cab tomorrow so I could bring my personal equipment and sending him the bill."

"What did he say to that?" Sambit asked, grinning at the idea of Derek handing his boss a cab bill.

"He told me to buy a car like a sane person."

"And?" Derek would never have let his boss have the last word.

"I offered to send him the bill for that instead."

Sambit laughed. "Did he agree to pay for the cab fare?"

"No, but he did say he'd pick me up in the morning."

"How did Fido do with you gone all day?"

"He's definitely glad to see me, but nothing's torn up and he didn't make any messes in his room, so I figure he did okay," Derek replied. "I'd love to take him with me the way I did when I was working with the National Guard, but I don't have a doggy seat for my motorcycle."

"Do you have a second helmet?" Sambit asked impulsively.

"Sure do," Derek drawled. "Wanna go for a ride?"

"Maybe someday," Sambit said, his courage deserting him.

"Just tell me when," Derek replied. "My bike is at your disposal."

"What about you?"

"You already know the answer to that," Derek reminded him. "Say the word and I'll be there in a couple of hours."

"I'm hoping the influx of new people tomorrow will mean I can start planning a graceful exit," Sambit admitted. "I've enjoyed the work—other than the stress of dealing with Tucker—but not the working conditions. I was telling Lyrica earlier that I might start looking for a job in industry. I've been in the classroom a long time, long enough to have forgotten how much I like doing what I teach about."

"I'll put a good word in for you at NASA," Derek said immediately. "It's not nepotism, or whatever you want to call it, because we wouldn't be working together except very indirectly. The nuclear power program is completely separate from the robotics program."

"Would you actually have any pull, then?" Sambit asked.

"Not directly," Derek said, "but I've worked there for about ten years. I know people, and I'm well enough known for my intolerance for any kind of bullshit that if I say you're good, they're likely to believe me, simply because I never say it unless I mean it. I can't make any promises, of course, but it can't hurt for me to mention you and your possible interest."

"I suppose not," Sambit said. "It wouldn't be until January at the earliest. I can't leave A&M in a lurch like that with only a few weeks' notice to find a replacement for my fall classes."

"Of course you can't," Derek agreed. "You're much too responsible and loyal for that. That doesn't mean you can't start looking, though."

It was exactly what Sambit had said to Lyrica.

"If you have any information on what they're looking for, could you send it to me?" Sambit asked. "Along with contact information or anything like that? I can send my résumé if nothing else."

"Sure," Derek said. "I'll have to ask Kenneth tomorrow who would be the best person to contact. As I said, I don't work with that division much. So, you gonna move in with me if you get a job at NASA? We can share the commute."

"We'll see," Sambit equivocated. "It's way too soon to commit to something like that."

"Why?" Derek asked. "Don't you believe in love at first sight?"

"Derek, I come from a country where eighty percent of all marriages are arranged for the couple by their families, maybe even more. Love doesn't enter the equation."

"You don't believe in love?"

"I didn't say that," Sambit said with a sigh, "just that I'm not used to basing decisions on that criterion. A relationship isn't about emotions. Emotions are as variable as the day and the hour. Relationships are about commitment and about choices, about choosing to do what's best for the other person even when you're tired or angry or not particularly in love with them, and that isn't a commitment you should make rashly."

"That almost makes sense," Derek said. "Almost. It's not how I'm used to thinking, but I could get behind that, I think. I can certainly say I never felt like my past boyfriends made an effort to follow that philosophy, and I can probably trace that to the relationship failing. Of course, I can't say I was any better. Life has sort of demanded I look out for number one."

"I'm not saying you shouldn't look out for yourself," Sambit said. "You can't do what's best for your partner if you aren't in good shape yourself, but I've seen too many relationships descend to a level of deliberately doing things to hurt the other person because you aren't committed fully or out of spite or whatever, and that doesn't belong in a healthy relationship."

"So would you consider ours a healthy relationship?" Derek asked.

"I...." Sambit had to stop to think about it. The idea that they were actually *in* a relationship was still so new to him that it was hard to see past that to the dynamics between them. "I guess I would," he said finally. "I mean, it's hard since we aren't together. We aren't really making a lot of decisions that impact each other directly. Not like if we were living together."

"I see."

"Wait," Sambit said. "Why are you angry?"

"I'm not angry," Derek said, although the clipped tone of his voice belied his words. "A little hurt that you don't consider all the texts and calls and e-mails making decisions that might impact you. I can stop if you'd prefer I not send them."

"No!" Sambit's heart raced at the thought of losing Derek through his own stupidity, never mind that he wasn't sure it wouldn't happen for other reasons. "I don't want you to stop. Lyrica's been telling me for a week now that I was letting my own baggage get in the way of giving you a fair chance. I should have listened sooner. I'm sorry."

Derek waited so long to reply that Sambit wondered if he'd hung up. "Are you still there?"

"Yeah," Derek said finally. "I'm trying to take your advice from earlier and make choices based on what I promised us both I'd do rather than on the way I'm feeling right now. It's not easy."

"I told you relationships were hard work," Sambit quipped, trying to lighten the mood. "But if we've had our first fight, we can have our first makeup sex."

Derek snorted softly. "Not tonight. I'm not ending things, so don't get that in your head, but I think maybe we need a few days' break. I'll take this relationship as seriously as you want, but you have to meet me halfway. If we aren't on the same page, one of us is going to end up hurt, and I don't want that to happen to either of us."

"So what do you want me to do?" Sambit asked uneasily.

"I want you to think about what you want from me," Derek said. "When you can answer that question, you know how to reach me."

"Okay," Sambit said, not knowing what else to say. "If that's what you want."

"It isn't what I want at all," Derek admitted, "but I think it's what we both need."

chapter
SIXTEEN

robotech: How's Sambit? Is he having headaches still?

Derek waited on pins and needles for Lyrica's reply to his chat message. It had been four days since their "fight," if that was even the right name for it. Four days since he'd told Sambit to think about what he wanted their relationship to mean and to call Derek when he'd figured it out. Four days of silence.

sopsolo: Miserable, but no headaches. Call him.

robotech: I can't. The ball's in his court now. If he doesn't want me, I won't force him into something.

sopsolo: *snort* Not want you? You two are something else. He's moped around here for four days looking like his favorite pet died and you've resorted to bothering me to find out how he is. Pathetic. Really.

It probably was, but Derek wasn't about to agree with Lyrica on that point. If he did, she'd double her insistence that Derek call Sambit immediately and put an end to this ridiculous standoff. As much as Derek wanted to do just that, he couldn't be the one to make the call. That had to come from Sambit. Derek had to know Sambit was as invested in making a relationship work as he was, because if Sambit wasn't, this wouldn't be any different than all the other failed attempts in his past. Derek had enough of those. He didn't need another one. He especially didn't need to be the one chasing after his lover like a lovesick puppy. He had more self-respect than that, and besides, Sambit wouldn't respect him for it either.

robotech: I know how it must look, but he hadn't even gotten to the point of thinking about us as a couple. I poured my heart into my e-mails. I did everything I could think of to convince him I was serious.

sopsolo: Ask him about Praveen the next time you talk to him.

robotech: Who?

sopsolo: Ask Sambit. It's not my story to tell, but it'll all make more sense then.

robotech: Just tell me. Please?

sopsolo: Fine. You'll still have to get the details from him, but Sambit tried the long-distance thing once before, when he first came to the US. The guy dumped him to get married within a month and didn't have the courtesy to tell Sambit the truth himself. Sambit had to hear it from his mother.

robotech: Shit.

sopsolo: Yes, exactly.

It made a little more sense to Derek now, the insistence that long-distance relationships couldn't work. That didn't mean Sambit was right or that Derek appreciated being tarred with the same brush as Sambit's ex, but at least it explained Sambit's near fanaticism on the subject.

robotech: So I guess you think I should call him.

sopsolo: You know I do.

robotech: I'll think about it.

He'd done nothing but think about it, honestly, but he wasn't going to tell Lyrica that. His boss had even noticed, asking him why he was so distracted. Derek had brushed it off and asked Kenneth about the nuclear power division instead. Maybe he'd e-mail Sambit tomorrow from work with that information. It wouldn't be from his personal e-mail so he wouldn't include anything but the information he'd promised Sambit, but hopefully it would be enough to remind Sambit that he kept his promises. If Sambit started to believe that, maybe he'd believe the rest and give Derek the chance to keep the rest of the promises he'd made.

Yes, he'd do that in the morning. Sambit would find it when he got off work tomorrow evening, and maybe he'd call.

robotech: How are the new additions working out?

sopsolo: Most of them are pretty good, but nobody with much robotics experience. Tucker screwed up when he sent you home. That's the other good news. He's being replaced next week. Of course, I suppose the new guy could be as bad as Tucker, but we can hope anyway.

robotech: That's good. I hope you'll be less stressed with him gone.

sopsolo: You mean you hope Sambit will be less stressed.

robotech: That too, but I really don't want you to be stressed either. I think of you as one of my friends too, you know.

sopsolo: I know. I was teasing.

robotech: Well don't. I'm not in the mood at the moment.

sopsolo: Call Sambit.

robotech: Tell him to call me.

sopsolo: What do you think I've been doing for the last four days? He's as stubborn as you are. Call him.

He couldn't talk about it anymore, but he wasn't quite ready to deal with an empty house and no human contact for the evening.

robotech: so what's with the IM handle? sopsolo?

sopsolo: I'm the soprano soloist in the local community choir. With a name like Lyrica, you knew I was going to be a musician of some sort.

robotech: Oh, cool. Let me know next time you perform. I'd love to come see you.

sopsolo: As long as you bring Sambit with you.

Derek sighed. Lyrica wasn't letting it go.

robotech: If he's talking to me again by then, I will. I'm going to do some laundry and take Fido for a walk.

sopsolo: I'll tell him you asked about him.

robotech: You'll do no such thing. He'll call me or not when he's ready. Don't interfere.

That was probably wishful thinking, but he had to say it anyway. He logged out of chat before she could reply and tempt him again with calling Sambit. "Come on, Fido," he called, grabbing the leash. "Let's go for a walk."

The dog bounded up to him, tongue lolling and tail wagging excitedly at the thought of a walk. "I'm glad someone still wants to be with me."

That wasn't fair to Sambit, and he knew it, but it was hard to keep his hopes up when he hadn't talked to Sambit in four days.

They walked the circular route around his neighborhood. Derek smiled at the sight of piles of trash on the curb. As disturbing as it was to know that much had been damaged, it was proof of people coming back and picking up the threads of their lives again, and that was a source of hope.

One of Derek's neighbors, a man he recognized on sight but didn't know by name, came out of his house dragging a big roll of carpet.

"Flooded?" Derek asked sympathetically.

"Only about two inches of water," the man called back, "but enough to ruin the carpet. I'm not going to complain too much, though. The roof didn't fall in like a lot of the other houses did. My wife's been after me to tear the carpet out now that the kids are grown and put down hardwoods. I guess she's going to get her wish."

"What a good way to look at it," Derek said with a laugh.

The man laughed too. "Next time I'll do what she wants without the storm to make me, I think."

"Good idea," Derek said. "If I never live through another storm like that one, it'll be too soon."

"Did you have a lot of damage?"

"Not too much," Derek said. "Certainly not like a lot of people seem to have. It makes me glad I put all the upgrades into the house when it was being built. They paid off."

The man nodded. "Yeah, we did the same thing. We'll have some shingles to replace, but other than the water and downed branches, we seem okay. We're having an inspector come out to check the foundation since we know we had water in the house, and the insurance inspector has already looked at the interior damage. Thank goodness for flood insurance."

"Really!" Derek agreed, though he hadn't needed it this time. After seeing the damage in his neighborhood, he wouldn't let it lapse anytime soon. Fido pulled impatiently at the leash. "I'd better finish his walk before he finishes me. Good luck with the redecorating."

Fido whined a little when they passed the house where Derek had found him, but the dog made no attempt to go toward the house, much to Derek's relief. He couldn't see any sign that the owners had returned. No pile of trash waited for pickup, whenever city services were restored. No lights shone through the remaining windows, and no boards covered the broken ones. Wherever Fido's old owners were, they weren't here, and that was fine with Derek.

"SO WHY haven't you called Derek yet?"

Sambit opened his eyes, blinking a couple of times to help them adjust to the sudden brightness in the room. "Why are you in my trailer?"

"Because you and Derek are both being fools and I'm tired of it," Lyrica said. "You're moping around like someone kicked your puppy, and he's texting me instead of texting you, and this is getting ridiculous. You're grown men, not prepubescent boys with no sense. So why haven't you called Derek yet?"

"Because he doesn't want me."

"Like hell! I just spent twenty minutes in a chat window assuring him you were as miserable as he was and that you hadn't died of radiation poisoning and everything else I could think of to try to make him feel better about the fact that you hadn't called. That man is stupid with wanting you."

"Then why did he tell me not to call him?"

Lyrica let out a huge sigh. "God, why do men have to make everything so complicated?" She plopped down on the mattress of the narrow metal bed that had replaced the army cot. "What did he tell you? Exactly."

"He said not to call him."

"Ever? Then why is he telling me he's waiting for you to call?"

"Not never," Sambit said. "Until I could tell him what I wanted out of our relationship, but there is no relationship, so how am I supposed to know what I want?"

"I give up," Lyrica said, standing up and glaring at him. "He's told you he considers it a relationship. He's told me he considers it a relationship. I've told you it looks like every relationship I've ever seen except for the fact that you aren't together at the moment, but that's temporary. If you keep going like this, you're going to be right, and it's not going to be because he didn't want you. It's going to be because you pushed him away so often that he stopped coming back for more rejection. He's being patient with you at the moment. He's waiting for you to call him, but if you don't put some effort into nurturing that, even if you e-mail him and tell him you're still thinking or that you need to wait until you get home or something, if you don't let him know you still want him, he is going to get tired of waiting eventually, and then all your self-fulfilling prophecies will have come true through no fault of anyone but you. Is that what you want?"

Sambit sighed. "No."

"Then why won't you do anything to change it?"

"Because I don't know how to answer him."

"Of all the stupid things."

"I'm getting a little tired of you calling me stupid," Sambit complained.

"Then stop acting stupid and I won't have to call you on it," Lyrica retorted. "This isn't nuclear physics. It's a relationship. What would make you happy?"

What would make him happy? Sambit had gotten so used to simply accepting his life as it was that he wasn't sure he knew what happy was anymore. "I liked hearing about his day," he said finally. "I liked telling him about mine."

"That's a good start. What else?"

"I liked joking with him."

"What else?"

"I don't know," Sambit said, his hands shaking with frustration. "All the relationships I've ever been in have failed."

"Why?"

"What?"

"Why have all your relationships failed?" Lyrica said. "What went wrong, and how do you keep that from happening with Derek?"

"I told you about Praveen."

"So distance was the problem there," Lyrica said, "and you're still gun-shy from that, especially since Derek doesn't live down the street from you, but I'd be willing to bet there were a few other factors, like family and societal pressure."

"Yes, probably."

"You don't have to worry about those," Lyrica said. "Derek's about as out and proud as they come. I can't swear nobody's pressuring him, but I'd put good money on him not caving to it."

Sambit couldn't argue with that. Derek made absolutely no bones about his preference for his own gender.

"So what else?" Lyrica prompted when Sambit didn't continue. "What else went wrong?"

"Do we have to talk about this?"

"No, we don't have to talk about it, but you have to think about it," Lyrica insisted. "Ignoring it will make it go away, but it won't solve anything."

"If I promise to think about it, will you stop talking about it?"

"Yes, but whatever you decide, you have to call Derek," Lyrica said. "Even if it's to tell him that you don't want to see him again, that you don't care enough about him to give a relationship a chance, don't do to him what Praveen did to you."

"That's a low blow."

"Maybe, but it's what you're doing. You're leaving him hanging, waiting to hear from you, hoping everything will work out. If it doesn't, that's fine, but don't leave him in the dark. Whatever you decide, be man enough to tell him yourself."

"Fine," Sambit said. "I will. Just drop it now."

Lyrica didn't look convinced, but she left him alone with his dark thoughts. Despite his answers to Lyrica, he had been thinking about Derek's question. He missed the e-mails, the texts, the phone calls. He missed the connection, however tenuous. He missed the flirting and the phone sex, but more than that, he missed telling Derek about his day and feeling like the other man was genuinely interested in hearing what Sambit had to say.

So what did he want from Derek?

The easy answer would have been a life together, but Sambit didn't see it being possible. Derek would never agree to be discreet about their relationship. He'd want to go with Sambit to university events and temple functions, and he'd want Sambit to go with him to events for the staff at NASA. Sambit didn't mind that part quite so much, that being Derek's life and friends, not his own, but Sambit didn't know how his colleagues would react if he brought Derek with him to the faculty picnic or to convocation or any such events. A&M had their own version of a Gay Straight Alliance, but Sambit had never paid any attention to how active they were or how they were received on campus by either the students or the other faculty. It hadn't mattered because he hadn't planned on bringing anyone to campus with him. If he got together with Derek, he wouldn't have a choice, not if he wanted to keep Derek for more than a fling.

It would mean turning his entire life upside down, and while he was tempted in a way he'd never been tempted before, fear held him back. If it didn't work out, he'd be left without even Derek's companionship to make up for the changes.

He'd never had a relationship last past a month or two. With that kind of track record, he was hardly optimistic now. At least he'd be able to go home soon. Tucker's replacement, a sensible man named Davis, had found someone who could run and repair the robots, and with the influx of new people to work on decommissioning the plant, Sambit would only be needed for another week. He'd be home in time for the end of summer faculty picnic. That would help him settle back into his real life, and everything would feel more balanced after that.

Lyrica's words about Praveen echoed in his head. He picked up his phone and texted Derek.

I haven't forgotten you. I just need a little more time.

chapter
SEVENTEEN

SAMBIT'S apartment seemed incredibly quiet after the near-constant buzz of noise at the power plant in Bay City. He told himself he should be glad of the peace, but instead he missed the companionship. He gave himself a day to be lazy; then he did all his laundry, cleaned the apartment from one end to the other, and revised his syllabus for the fall semester based on his experiences over the summer. He also made a note to discuss adding a basic robotics engineering course to the requirements for a degree in applied nuclear engineering.

That kept him busy through the night before the faculty picnic. He tossed and turned all night, vague dreams of showing up at the picnic in only his boxers mixed with dreams of showing up with Derek and being run off by his jeering peers.

When he awoke, he told himself that was ridiculous. They were all too professional to jeer at him as they had in his dreams. They would politely shun him, and that would be worse.

He sighed and made himself go through his normal morning routine: yoga, tea with real milk instead of the awful creamer packets they'd had at the power plant, chana masala and poori for breakfast, and then answering e-mails. The last e-mail he'd gotten from Derek stared at him accusingly as he worked, the one from his NASA address with information about who to contact about a possible job. An e-mail that had arrived even after he'd sent the last text to Derek two weeks ago asking for more time. He owed Derek an answer. He knew that, but he couldn't seem to come to a decision. He missed the other man terribly, but he still didn't see how it could be anything more than a pipe dream.

He answered all the other e-mail in his inbox, leaving only the one from Derek. He'd think about it after he got back from the faculty picnic that afternoon. He needed a shower and then he needed to head out, since the picnic wasn't in College Station but out on one of the ranches surrounding town. He might joke about Indian time, but he hated to be late to anything.

He debated what to wear but finally decided on jeans and a polo shirt. He'd probably be hot, but he couldn't make himself wear shorts to a university function, even one as casual as the picnic.

He wasn't the first person to arrive when he got to the ranch at a few minutes after noon, but he didn't need to be first, just not late. He summoned a smile and a handshake for his colleagues, asking about their summers and saying as little as possible about his. The hurricane was a huge topic of conversation, needless to say, as well as the near-miss with the meltdown in Bay City.

"Have you been following the developments at the South Texas nuclear plant?" Peter Jones, one of Sambit's colleagues, asked.

"Closely," Sambit said. "It's an interesting case, made more complicated, from what I understand, by the NRC representative who disagreed with the local team on what the outcome should be. In a year or two, when it isn't quite so fresh in people's minds, I think it could make an interesting case study. The other thing I found interesting was the use of robots once again to do work in situations that were unsafe for humans. I wonder if we're doing our students a disservice by not requiring them to learn at least some basic robotics."

"Is there such a thing?" Peter asked. "I mean, that's an entire field in itself. How do we add that to an already heavy course load?"

"I wasn't thinking as much about the creation of robots as I was about the maintenance of them," Sambit admitted. "A NASA robotics engineer created the robots being used at the plant, but the people on site were expected to maintain them, and they found that to be outside their abilities beyond the very basics."

"You really have been following it closely," Peter said. "Where did you get your information? I thought I'd searched pretty thoroughly, but I missed that."

Sambit sighed. "I was there until about three days ago helping contain the situation, but I'd rather that stay quiet. I don't want people thinking I'm playing at being a hero."

"Somehow I don't think there was any playing involved."

"Sambit, Peter, come meet our new biogenetics faculty."

Eager to escape the conversation with Peter, Sambit joined the head of the physics department. "Sambit Patel, Dr. Bradley Smith-Wallace, lately arrived from University of Maine. He'll be setting up a genetics lab and teaching some of our advanced bio courses."

"Nice to meet you," Sambit said, offering his hand. "Bradley, was it?"

"Please, call me Brad. The only person who calls me Bradley is my mother."

"And you don't want to meet his mother," another man said, joining them and giving Brad a fond smile.

"Be nice," Brad scolded. "My mother is coming around. Dr. Patel, this is my husband, Paul Smith-Wallace."

Sambit felt the world tilt on its axis as he shook the other man's hand. The new bio professor was gay, married, and completely unconcerned about the reaction of the rest of the faculty. Furthermore, no one hearing the introduction seemed to care. "Nice to meet you," Sambit said automatically. "Are you in genetics also?"

Paul laughed. "Oh, God, no! I'm an interior designer. I know, call it cliché, but I have a good sense of space, light, and color. It was either that or be an artist, and I had to pay the bills somehow. Unlike some people, I'm not independently wealthy."

It was obviously a familiar dig given the indulgent look on Brad's face, but it wasn't their interactions that made Sambit's chest hurt. It was Derek's absence. If he hadn't been such an idiot, he could be standing here right now introducing his partner as well.

"Have you been married long?" Sambit asked.

"Not as long as we would've liked," Paul said. "Maine hadn't approved gay marriage when we started dating, but while we jumped at the opportunity to make it legal, there anyway, since Texas doesn't recognize it, we still celebrate the anniversary of moving in together as well as our wedding anniversary."

"Well, congratulations either way," Sambit said. "I look forward to working with Brad and hopefully with getting to know you both better." He took a deep breath and plowed on. "It will be nice not to be the only faculty member with a same-sex partner."

"Oh, that would be nice!" Paul said. "Is your partner here?"

"Not today," Sambit said. "He works at NASA, and the storm has his schedule all messed up. I'm hoping he'll be at some of the orientation events with me, though. We'll have to see." He'd have to see if he'd convinced Derek to forgive him for being an idiot and take another chance on him between now and then, but even if he couldn't, Brad would know he wasn't alone on the faculty, and maybe Sambit would have two new friends.

He spent the rest of the picnic plotting ways to convince Derek to take him back, but everything he came up with seemed either extravagant or ludicrous. He wasn't any closer to a plan when he left than when he'd started except for one thing.

As soon as he was in his car, he pulled out his cell phone and texted Derek. *Send me your address, please. I have to see you. I can be there in two hours.*

Derek's text came back with gratifying quickness, giving the Pearland address. Sambit programmed it into his GPS and texted back the estimated time of arrival.

The drive through Houston seemed to take forever, even though he arrived at Derek's house a few minutes before the estimated time he'd given. He found the house easily, one of the few on the block with light streaming through the windows in welcome. Even in the fading light of the day, Sambit could see the destruction wrought by the storm and the first signs of recovery in the light shining through various windows. Sambit parked and locked his car, stumbling over the usually routine details in his nervousness, but delaying wouldn't gain him anything. He knocked on the front door and waited.

Fido's barking greeted him before Derek got there, making Sambit smile. He was glad Derek had managed to keep the dog. It was a small thing to worry about compared to all the problems of rebuilding a city and a relationship, but it was an easy one to focus on. Then the door opened and Derek stood before him, backlit by the light in the foyer. "I'm sorry it took me so long to call. I'm sorry it took me so long to figure out what I wanted. I'm sorry it took me this long to realize I'm ready for the hard work."

The words babbled out of him, completely unscripted, unordered, nothing like his usual controlled speech, but Derek didn't seem to mind. He grabbed Sambit's hand, pulling him inside and into a kiss that stole what little coherency remained after his garbled speech. Sambit held tight and returned the kiss with all the desperation of six weeks of separation and three weeks of silence.

"You're here," Derek murmured, lifting his head finally. "You're actually here. I wanted to believe you would be, but...."

"But it took me a long time to get my head on straight," Sambit finished. "I'm sorry. Will you let me make it up to you?"

"I'm sure I can think of something," Derek replied with that mischievous grin that went straight to Sambit's groin.

Sambit slid a hand between them, feeling bolder than he ever had, and stroked Derek's burgeoning erection. "I'm sure you can," he agreed. "Hands, mouth, you name it."

"Ass?" Derek asked.

"If you want it," Sambit said, swallowing hard at the thought. "I meant what I said."

"Maybe we'll work up to that," Derek said. "I wouldn't have the patience tonight anyway. It's all I can do not to jump you right now."

"I'm not stopping you," Sambit said, stroking Derek again, "but I owe you an explanation too."

"Later," Derek said, tugging Sambit deeper into the house. "After we get naked."

That sounded like a fine idea to Sambit. He followed along behind Derek eagerly, with Fido at their heels. "Go to your room," Derek told the dog. To Sambit's surprise, the dog listened, padding off in the opposite direction. Derek led Sambit through the living room to a narrow hallway that led into a large master suite decorated in rich browns and greens, a beautifully masculine room for a beautiful, masculine man. If he hadn't been so ridiculously grateful to be there, he might have teased Derek about the matching comforter, pillows, and window treatments, but he was too happy with his current situation to do anything that might change Derek's mind.

Another time Sambit would linger with the preliminaries, undressing Derek carefully, lingering over each patch of skin that was revealed, but he didn't have the patience for that tonight, and neither did Derek, if the speed with which his clothes went flying across the room was any indication. Sambit followed suit, stripping down to his boxers as quickly as he could. When he looked up to see Derek sliding his own shorts over his gorgeous backside, Sambit figured that was an invitation and dropped his as well. "I want to lick you all over."

Derek's eyebrows lifted in surprise, but Sambit was too turned on to care if his words were uncharacteristically bold. His mouth watered at the thought of all that skin just waiting to be explored and Derek's cock at the end of it, the perfect treat to end his day. "Just don't pin me down, okay?"

The vulnerability in Derek's comment brought Sambit up short. Yes, he wanted Derek like crazy, could practically taste the fluid seeping from the tip of his erection already, but he didn't want to make Derek uncomfortable. "We can do something else. I don't want you to have to fight bad memories the whole time I'm trying to make love to you."

"It's not like that," Derek said. "Most of the time I don't even think about it. I just take charge, and it doesn't matter."

"Let's do it this way," Sambit suggested, climbing on Derek's bed and urging Derek to straddle him. He scooted down until his shoulders were between Derek's legs. "There. Now you're on top, you're in control, and I get what I want too."

"I have an even better idea," Derek said, flipping around so he faced Sambit's feet. "Now we can both get what we want."

Sambit was sure this was a bad idea. He'd never be able to give Derek the attention he deserved if Derek was sucking him at the same time, but refusing wasn't an option either, not when Derek was already blowing cool air over Sambit's heated skin. Resolving to employ all the control yoga had taught him, he focused on returning the pleasure

Derek had lavished on him before, starting with the heavy sac hanging in his face.

At the unusual angle, it probably wasn't the smoothest blow job Sambit had ever given, but as Derek started moving, his cock sliding in and out of Sambit's mouth and then down into his throat, his own mouth moving over Sambit's length with the same desperate rhythm, Sambit decided it was his favorite and that he had a new favorite position. He clung to Derek's hips, not to guide him but simply to add one more layer of connection, the skin smooth beneath his palms. Then Derek moved his head, his lips leaving Sambit's cock to move lower, over Sambit's balls. One long finger pressed against Sambit's entrance. His whole body clenched, half in anticipation, half in rejection. He hadn't been touched that way in so long. Derek backed off after that, his hands still holding Sambit's cheeks, spreading them the tiniest bit but not moving into the crease. Sambit trembled, every muscle in his body pulled taut with sensual tension. He tried to focus on his breathing, to control his body's reactions as yoga had taught him to do, so he could draw out their encounter that much longer, but the flavor of Derek's cock on his tongue, the occasional waft of breath over his entrance, and the immense sensation of being beneath and surrounded by Derek were too much for his willpower. He bent his knees and lifted his hips, offering his body to Derek in any way the other man wanted, increasing the suction of his lips at the same time. He might not be able to slow down his reactions, but he could do his best to take Derek with him when he climaxed.

Derek's hips moved jerkily beneath Sambit's hands, signaling his impending release. Sambit relaxed his throat and let Derek move as he needed to. He closed his eyes to better appreciate the sensation of Derek's mouth on him, but that deprived him of the sight of Derek's ass bouncing in front of him.

He could feel his release building, pent-up need that all the masturbation in the world couldn't satisfy, need for the man above him, pushing to get free. Sambit squeezed Derek's hand in warning, the position of their bodies such that he couldn't get his mouth free. Derek seemed to understand, squeezing Sambit's hand in return and moving his head to lick Sambit's balls while continuing the erotic stimulation with his hand.

Sambit cried out around his mouthful as his orgasm exploded out of him, covering his belly and Derek's hand. Seconds later, Derek started to pull away, but Sambit grabbed his hips, holding him in place. Sambit understood why Derek had moved his head, but Sambit didn't have the same hesitations. He wanted Derek to come in his mouth. He wanted that flavor on his tongue.

He got his wish.

When they could both breathe again, Derek turned back around so he lay next to Sambit on the bed, his hand stroking up and down Sambit's arm leisurely. "So you changed your mind, huh?"

"Not so much changed it as realized what was there all along," Sambit said. "I was at the end of summer picnic for the faculty, missing you anyway, and then suddenly my boss introduced me to the new bio prof and his husband."

"*His* husband?" Derek repeated.

"Brad and Paul Smith-Wallace," Sambit confirmed. "They're from Maine. They were there at the picnic together, and the world didn't end."

"And you were afraid it would?" Sambit could hear Derek's amusement in his voice.

"I grew up in an environment where in any kind of public or professional setting, you were expected to be uniformly asexual," Sambit struggled to explain. "Not that people didn't bring their spouses to work-related social events, but it was different. I don't really know how to put it in words except to say that it was very hard for me to conceive of showing up at an event like that with you at my side."

"And yet you're here," Derek said, "so how is this going to work?"

"We talked for a few minutes, and I told them I was glad not to be the only professor with a same-sex partner. I don't know what will happen. I don't know that I'll ever be comfortable with the kind of activism you believe in, but I'm done hiding."

Derek waited so long to answer that Sambit was afraid he'd somehow scared Derek off with his declaration. When he turned to look, Derek's eyes shimmered with emotion. Sambit rolled to his side, stroking Derek's hair back from his temples and kissing him tenderly. "Will you give me a second chance?"

"You're still on your first chance," Derek said, his voice rough with emotion. "I hadn't quite gotten to the point of giving up yet."

"Don't," Sambit said. "Don't ever give up on me, okay? I know we have things to work out, like the fact that we live two hours apart, but we were making it work when I was still at the power plant until I freaked out on you. I should probably explain that."

"That's up to you," Derek said. "I'll listen anytime you want to talk about it, but I know how hard it is to share the scars life leaves on us."

"I came to the US at twenty-two," Sambit explained, "fresh out of college and full of plans. I was going to get my PhD so I could get a good job in India. I would earn enough money that I'd take away the only real threat my parents could make to try to force me into an arranged marriage. That way Praveen and I could be together, and even if our families disowned us, we'd be okay."

"Obviously that didn't work out since you're still here," Derek said.

"No, it didn't work out. I thought Praveen was as committed to our path as I was. A month after I got here, my mother called to tell me the wonderful news. My good friend Praveen was getting married the following weekend to the mayor's daughter," Sambit said. "He was from a wealthier family than I was, and I underestimated the influence they could bring to bear on his life. I swore to myself right then that I'd never have another long-distance relationship. If a lover wanted to leave me, that was fine, but he'd have to do it to my face rather than behind my back like Praveen did."

"I don't have that great a track record when it comes to relationships," Derek said, "but I swear I'll never do something like that to you. We may argue. We may even break up someday. I can't see the future so I don't know what it holds, but I swear I will never disappear without an explanation. If things end—and I hope they won't, so don't misunderstand me—I will do it honestly and to your face."

"I know that," Sambit said. "Whatever I may have thought or feared, it wasn't that you'd treat me the way Praveen did, but the whole experience, besides turning me off long-distance relationships, left me feeling...."

"Unattractive?" Derek suggested. "Unlovable?"

"Not to mention incapable of holding a lover's interest," Sambit admitted.

"You don't know that was the problem at all," Derek insisted. "And even if it was, it could have been his problem, not yours."

"How could it have been his problem?" Sambit asked.

"I don't know," Derek was, "but I'm sure it was. I think you're fascinating, so there was obviously something wrong with him."

Sambit laughed. "You're just saying that because you want to get me in bed."

Derek made a show of looking around the room, even pushing up on his elbow and lifting the covers so he could see their nude bodies pressed together. "Baby, I already did that. Now if you'd said that I wanted to keep you in bed, you'd be right."

Sambit laughed. "Incorrigible."

"Irresistible," Derek said with a smile. "Kind of pointless to deny it."

Sambit shook his head and kissed Derek again. "So, um, I mentioned the couple I met at the picnic today."

"The ones you came out to," Derek said. "Yes, and I don't think I told you how proud of you I am."

"Well, I sort of told them I had a boyfriend," Sambit said. "That was about the time I realized I wanted you, whatever it took. I told them you weren't there because you had to work today. I hope you don't mind."

"I don't mind," Derek said. "I'm glad you think of me that way, even if you didn't tell me first. We should do something with them sometime. Dinner or a movie or something."

"Really? You'd want to do things like that with me?"

"It's what couples do, Sam."

"I know, but I've never really had that before. We'll have to work out the details, but maybe you and Fido could come spend the weekend at my place sometimes, and we could have them over for dinner or something."

Derek yawned. "We'll work out the details, but can we do it tomorrow? It's time to sleep now, and I can't think of anything better than having you sleep in my arms."

How was he supposed to resist that? He wasn't, he decided, curling deeper into Derek's arms and closing his eyes. He was asleep within seconds.

chapter
EIGHTEEN

"NEXT time we're totally inviting people to my house," Derek said. "Your whole living area is smaller than my kitchen."

"Don't rub it in," Sambit said. "We aren't all rich industry engineers."

"You could be," Derek said. "One job was filled, but they posted another one as I was leaving work yesterday. You're a shoo-in if you want it."

"We'll see." Sambit didn't really think of it as hedging his bets. He and Derek had managed to see each other every weekend since the memorable faculty picnic and its aftermath, and they talked on the phone every night they weren't together. Sambit's doubts were fading in the light of Derek's obvious and continuing interest and determination to make things work between them. Leaving a job he loved, though, was a huge step, one he wasn't quite sure he was ready to take. Working at the power plant had reminded him of the pleasures of hands-on work, but he had two juniors who had approached him soon after the start of school about mentoring them through their senior projects. Their enthusiasm reminded him why he had started teaching in the first place, and it felt wrong to agree to help them only to leave at the end of their first year. He would find someone to help them if he did, but he hated not following through on his commitments.

"When we know them better, we'll think about asking them to drive two hours instead of ten minutes," Sambit said instead of discussing the job opportunity. "How's the sambar coming?"

"This recipe is fucked up. Who puts 'cook until it smells right' in a recipe?"

"My mother," Sambit deadpanned.

Derek flushed so adorably Sambit had to kiss him.

The doorbell rang, forestalling any further discussion. Sambit went to answer it, grinning still at Derek's sheepish look as he yelled at Fido in the bedroom to be quiet. Sambit chose not to tell Derek that he found his mother's recipes as frustrating at times as Derek did, but he had yet to find a recipe in a cookbook anywhere that tasted as good as hers, however inexact, not to mention that he couldn't find a lot of her signature dishes in cookbooks anywhere. They were too local to have a broader appeal. That hadn't stopped Derek from devouring every dish Sambit had ever put in front of him.

"Hello," Sambit said, opening the door for Brad and Paul. "Come in. Derek is in the kitchen."

"Oh, he cooks, does he?" Brad said. "Lucky you."

"He's trying out a new recipe tonight," Sambit said, "so we have to hope it'll be good."

"Oh, what are we having?" Paul asked.

"His mother's sambar if I can figure out this recipe," Derek grumbled, coming in from the kitchen. "Derek Marshall. Nice to meet you."

"Paul Smith-Wallace," Paul said, shaking Derek's hand. "Sambit mentioned you at the picnic. We were sorry not to get to meet you then."

"I had to work," Derek replied smoothly, "but I'm looking forward to more faculty functions. It's always fun to rile up the natives."

Paul laughed. "I suppose Texas isn't known for its tolerance, although we've been well received at the university so far."

"University campuses tend to be a little more open-minded than the average Podunk town," Brad said. "Brad Smith-Wallace."

"Welcome, both of you," Derek said. "I do have to keep an eye on dinner so it doesn't burn. Sam told me when we first met that I had to learn to make sambar if I wanted to keep him."

Sambit had said no such thing, but he didn't bother correcting Derek. It made a good story if nothing else, and Derek had proven to be a phenomenal cook, often reconstructing recipes from restaurants and improving on them. He couldn't wait to tell his mother what suggestions Derek had for her sambar.

DINNER passed amid much joviality. Derek found Paul and Brad to be men after his own heart, open and playful where their sexuality was concerned, not above a practical joke or two, and all-around enjoyable, friendly people. He was jealous as hell. Not that he doubted Sambit's dedication to their relationship, but Paul and Brad got to go home together every night. They got to share a bed at night and a breakfast table in the morning. They were the threads in each other's lives.

"How attached are you to this place?" Derek asked when Paul and Brad had left.

"It's faculty housing," Sambit said. "I'm not attached to it at all, but there's never been a reason to move anywhere else. Why?"

"Because I don't want to go home tomorrow night, but two hours is too much of a commute for every day," Derek said. "I think we should look for a place somewhere around Cypress. We'd each have an hour's drive that way, which would suck, but it would mean we'd be able to live together instead of only seeing each other on weekends."

"What about your house?" Sambit said. "You've put all that work into it."

Derek shrugged. "If you decide to take a job in industry, either at NASA or elsewhere, it might put you in town enough that we could move back into it together. With all the remodeling and rebuilding after the storm, I'm sure I'd have no trouble leasing it out in the meantime. And if you decide to continue teaching here, I'll sell it and we'll put the work into a new house together. It's a building. It's not irreplaceable."

"So, you want to move in together?"

"Don't you?" Derek asked. "We spend every weekend together. We talk all the time. I would've thought that was the next logical step."

"No, I mean, yes, it is," Sambit said quickly. "You just told me at one point that you had a really hard time sharing space with anyone. I thought that was a nice way of telling me we'd keep separate residences and keep going like we have been."

"I do have a hard time," Derek admitted. "I'm probably borderline OCD where things like that are concerned, but you're different. Having you at my house doesn't grate. Being here with you doesn't make me want to run back to my own safe place. We'll have to find someplace big enough for both of us and that will accept Fido if we rent or lease instead of buying."

"So does this mean you love me?" Sambit asked.

Derek froze. The words had come to mind more than once, but Sambit had been very clear on the matter. "I thought you didn't believe in love."

"I never said that," Sambit protested. "I said I didn't believe in love at first sight. I believe in a lasting affection based on common ground and mutual respect. I believe in choosing to spend your life with a person who makes you happy and whom you want to make happy. I just don't think you can know who that person is at first glance. We moved past first glance several months ago."

"So are you saying you love me?" Derek asked, not quite willing to put himself out there first, not in words anyway. He'd show how he felt in actions all day—and all night—long. He'd make love to Sambit until he screamed, fix him anything he wanted to eat, give him a backrub when he had a headache, and generally do anything he could to take care of his lover. Saying "I love you" was an entirely different matter.

"I'm saying that despite the obvious differences, we have enough common ground, mutual respect, and sheer stubbornness to make me want to give this a try."

"So you *do* love me!" Derek crowed. "It's fine. You don't have to say the words. It'll be our little secret."

"What about you?" Sambit pressed.

"Say you'll help me find a place in Cy-Fair where we can live together and I'll tell you."

"That's bribery."

"So?"

"So I don't believe in bribery."

"The same way you don't believe in love, huh? Move in with me, Sam?"

"Fine," Sambit huffed.

Derek tackled him, knocking him sideways onto the couch so he could cover Sambit's body with his own. "Yes, I love you. Don't make me say it again."

Sambit didn't reply, simply lifting his head and kissing Derek with such power and passion that Derek didn't need to hear the words. If Sambit kept kissing him that way, Derek might never need to hear them. He wormed his hands between them, pulling Sambit's shirt free from his pants so he could find skin. Sambit raked his hands down Derek's back, his fingernails biting even through the cloth. Derek hissed softly, rearing up to pull the polo over his head. Sambit leaned up and latched onto Derek's nipple. "Fuck," Derek said, his voice breaking on a groan. "Keep doing that."

Sambit didn't reply in words, but words during sex were overrated. Derek liked actions much better, especially when Sambit sucked harder and nipped at Derek's chest just the way he liked. Derek shifted on the couch, urging Sambit to spread his legs so Derek could rut against the juncture of his thighs. As hard as they both were, Derek figured this wouldn't take long. He wasn't quite willing to let it happen that fast, though, so he pulled away from Sambit's tempting mouth. "Too many clothes," he said, tugging at Sambit's belt.

"Pot, kettle," Sambit replied, popping the button on Derek's jeans.

It would be easy to strip and return to the same position and rub against Sambit until they came, but Derek wanted more than that tonight. He pulled Sambit's pants down, pushing them off his feet. "Turn over," he said, nudging Sambit's side and guiding him onto his hands and knees.

"What are you doing?" Sambit asked, his voice betraying a bit of concern.

"Not fucking you," Derek said. "We don't have lube or condoms, so stop worrying. I'll fuck you another time."

Sambit didn't relax, but Derek didn't wait. He figured he had one chance at this or else they'd be back to frottage on the couch. While he had nothing against frottage, tonight he wanted something a little more. Hoping to encourage a little more ease on Sambit's part, Derek slid his hands up his lover's back, stroking the supple skin and strong muscles. While his own skin was tanner than usual from the summer sun, he still looked starkly pale next to Sambit's dark complexion, a contrast that fascinated Derek. Bending so his body was draped over Sambit's, he pressed a kiss on Sambit's spine as high as he could reach, then slowly worked his way down Sambit's back, lingering over each vertebra. Sambit gasped and mewled softly, the sounds all Derek needed to know Sambit was enjoying his attentions. The tension seeped slowly from Sambit's body as Derek ministered to him. When Derek reached the base of Sambit's spine, he lingered, his hands massaging Sambit's cheeks, parting them every so often, preparing Sambit for the rest of what Derek had in mind. Finally Sambit's edginess faded, and he moved with Derek's caresses rather than remaining frozen in place. Taking that as his cue, Derek nudged Sambit forward onto his elbows as he licked his way down Sambit's crease to the dark hole nestled inside.

Sambit cried out so sharply that Derek lifted his head. "Don't tell me no one's ever rimmed you before."

"No one's ever rimmed me before."

"Then you're in for a treat," Derek promised. He took his time, lingering over the preliminaries, giving Sambit time to get used to the idea of Derek's tongue *on* his ass before he asked Sambit to get used to the idea of Derek's tongue *in* his ass. One step at a time, and all that.

Sambit tasted vaguely of sweat, but underneath that, Derek could smell his desire and just a whiff of Sambit's cologne, something that hinted of sandalwood and hot sultry nights in an Indian boudoir surrounded by silks and gold. Sambit would probably laugh at the image, but Derek found it incredibly arousing, with Sambit cast as the rajah and Derek as the supplicant come to beg the prince's favor. He wondered how Sambit felt about role playing, because Derek was thinking that sounded like a mighty fine idea. Like tomorrow.

First, though, he had to finish introducing his lover to this variation on oral sex. To that end, he narrowed the focus of his attentions, moving from the full length of Sambit's crease and even his balls to just the patch of skin around his entrance that clenched and jumped beneath Derek's tongue.

Little noises escaped from Sambit's lips as Derek continued to lavish pleasure on him, and then Derek rolled his tongue and speared it past the loosening entrance. Sambit cried out sharply, rearing up and dislodging Derek. He caught Sambit, pulling him against his chest, his cock slotting into the crease as he stroked Sambit's chest with tender hands. "Too much?"

Sambit shook his head, rutting back against Derek, riding his cock.

"Do you want to lean back over, or should I take care of you this way?" Derek asked, circling Sambit's cock with his fist.

Sambit pulsed his hips against Derek again, making him wish they had lube and condoms handy because he wanted inside that tight ass. That would wait for another night, though. They were both too wound up for that. Now that Sambit was pushing against him so wantonly, Derek wasn't sure he could pull back even to keep rimming his lover, so he took the choice from Sambit's hands, picking up a rhythm with his hand and hips designed to send them both soaring as quickly as possible.

Sambit was hot against him and beneath his hand, his skin burning with the same need that seared through Derek. "Come on, sweetheart," Derek urged. "Show me how much you love me."

"Sweetheart?" Sambit rasped. "Be careful or I'm going to start calling you sanam."

"Sunnem?" Derek repeated.

"Sanam. It's Hindi. It means darling."

"I like it. You can call me that anytime you want," Derek decided, licking Sambit's neck.

Sambit tipped his head to the side, encouraging Derek's caress, so Derek did it again, adding a hint of teeth this time, his hand still moving over Sambit's erection, keeping them both on edge. Sambit groaned at the gentle bite so Derek experimented again, a little harder this time. Sambit's cock jumped in his hand. Derek smiled and latched onto the curve of muscle, sucking and biting, determined to raise a mark that would be visible even on Sambit's mahogany skin. Within seconds Sambit convulsed beneath Derek's hands, slumping forward onto the couch again.

Derek followed him down, folding his body over Sambit's recumbent one, rubbing against the sweaty skin as he chased his own pleasure.

"Let me roll over," Sambit said, his breath still coming in harsh pants.

Derek pushed up onto his hands and knees so Sambit could roll beneath him, pulling Derek back down so Derek's hard cock pressed against Sambit's sated one. Derek kissed Sambit frantically as he rocked against his lover's body, the spurs of need sharp with the smell of Sambit's release fresh and hot between them.

Sambit broke their kiss and framed Derek's face with his hands. "Yes, I love you, sanam."

Derek dove back into the kiss, the words enough to break his control. He spurted between their bodies, his release mixing with Sambit's. All tension gone, he sagged against Sambit, relaxing into the arms that encircled him. "Every time you call me that, I'm going to remember you saying you love me."

"Good," Sambit said. "I hear it every time you call me Sam."

"I thought you hated that nickname."

"Not when you say it."

Derek smiled. "I love you, Sam."

EPILOGUE

"ARE you sure it's a good idea for me to come with you?" Derek asked.

Sambit had dragged him into Houston to Little Delhi to buy a new suit, and not just any suit, but a kurta pajama, an Indian suit with pants and an embroidered tunic. Part of Diwali, Sambit had explained, was wearing new clothes and cleaning your house and welcoming the goddess Lakshmi, who would bring wealth and goodness to her devotees. The goddess part was a bit too much for Derek, but he could get behind a clean house and an evening with friends and family, and if it meant he got to go with Sambit to the temple, he would even put on his kurta pajama and hope he didn't look as uncomfortable as he felt. Sambit and the shopkeeper had brought out suits of every jeweled shade for his approval, but Derek wasn't used to that much color and settled on a burnished gold tunic with simple maroon beading and embroidery accompanied by white pants. He still felt odd in the high collar with no tie or jacket, not that he really needed a coat in Houston at the end of October, but this was what Sambit insisted was traditional attire for this kind of event, and Derek was willing to do pretty much anything to make his lover happy.

Sambit hadn't felt any such constraints, choosing an outfit with a turquoise tunic, beaded at the neckline and sleeves and in small rosettes over the body of the garment, combined with scarlet trousers that matched the beading. It should have been garish, but against Sambit's dark skin, the colors popped. Sambit looked good enough to eat.

"So will there be a service?" Derek asked as they drove toward the temple.

"No, it's not that formalized," Sambit said. "We'll light the lamps, of course, but it's a time of gathering, of celebration. There will be food because no Indian event is complete without more food than ten times the number of guests could eat. It means so much to me that you'd come with me tonight, that you'd put on a kurta pajama even though you'd be more comfortable in an American suit, and that you'd be here with me."

"It's important to you, therefore it's important to me," Derek said with a shrug.

"And that is very precious to me, sanam."

Derek smiled. Sambit didn't say I love you very often, not that Derek said it much more, but he called Derek sanam regularly, and it never failed to make Derek smile.

Sambit had told Derek that Diwali was the festival of lights, but that hadn't prepared him for the sight that greeted him when they arrived at the temple. Strings of white lights covered the building so that it shone bright as day against the darkness. Cars filled the parking lot, and everyone getting out and going inside was dressed in the same vivid colors and fabrics as Sambit. Despite wearing Indian clothes, Derek felt positively plain in his muted gold tunic.

"You look very handsome," Sambit said, interrupting Derek's thoughts, "and everyone is going to see that you're wearing a kurta pajama and be thrilled that you're trying to fit in."

"They aren't going to look past the fact that we're together."

Sambit shrugged. "Their loss, not ours, but I've watched you charm people. You'll have them all eating out of the palm of your hand before long."

Derek hoped Sambit was right.

Inside the temple, it was absolute chaos, people milling around and greeting friends, setting up tables for the buffet and for eating. Oil lamps and candles glittered on every surface, casting the temple in a golden glow, the smoke from the lights mingling with the smoke from the incense to create a nearly overwhelming sensory experience. Derek didn't wait to be prompted, slipping his shoes off at the door. He and Sambit had talked about the proper way to greet the "aunties," as Sambit called them, the older ladies who made up the backbone of the temple no matter what their husbands liked to believe.

When Sambit introduced Derek to the first one to approach them, Derek stretched out his hands, palms touching prayer style, and offered them with a shallow bow. She covered his hands with hers in greeting. "Eliama Aunty, this is my partner, Derek Marshall."

"Pleased to meet you, ma'am," Derek said, his own upbringing kicking in.

"It's about time you brought someone with you to temple," Eliama scolded. "It's not good for a man to be alone."

The response was so completely the opposite of what Derek had feared that it took him a minute to respond. Sambit's expression betrayed equal surprise. "I wasn't sure how people would feel."

"Bah, they can feel what they want. I've watched you. You didn't look at the girls, you didn't accept the offers. You needed something else. If this man gives you that, then all is as it should be."

"Sukriya, Aunty."

Derek hadn't learned much Hindi beyond the endearment Sambit used, but he knew that one.

"Sukriya, Aunty," he echoed, wanting to add his own thanks to Sambit's. "I hope I'll be worthy of your faith in us."

"You're here, you're wearing a kurta pajama, you're barefoot. If you can eat with your fingers, all is good."

"You should taste his sambar," Sambit confided. "It's even better than my mother's."

"Don't let your mother hear you say that, or she'll disown you both."

"Yes, Aunty."

"Go eat, enjoy, celebrate. It's Diwali!"

The rest of the evening passed swiftly and in similar vein. If anyone had a problem with them being there together, they kept their opinions to themselves. Derek smiled at the aunty who offered him a fork and proceeded to eat his biryani with his hands just like everyone else.

As they were leaving, Derek stopped to look back at the temple and its denizens. "You know," he said slowly, "maybe next year I'll get that green outfit you wanted me to buy."

ARIEL TACHNA lives outside of Houston with her husband, her daughter and son, and their cat. Before moving there, she traveled all over the world, having fallen in love with both France, where she found her husband, and India, where she dreams of retiring someday. She's bilingual with snippets of four other languages to her credit and is as in love with languages as she is with writing.

Visit Ariel's website at http://www.arieltachna.com/ and her blog at http://arieltachna.livejournal.com/.

Also in ITALIAN

I SUOI DUE
PADRI

ARIEL
TACHNA

http://www.dreamspinnerpress.com

Also from ARIEL TACHNA

http://www.dreamspinnerpress.com

Also by ARIEL TACHNA

http://www.dreamspinnerpress.com

Contemporary Romance by ARIEL TACHNA

http://www.dreamspinnerpress.com

Also by ARIEL TACHNA

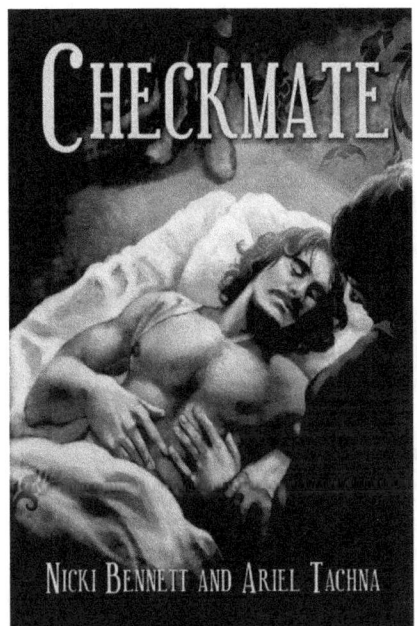